CW00428923

Sam

With of love and
best wishes.

TAILGATE

Billy McLaughlin

Available – The DI Phil Morris Mysteries

Lost Girl

In the Wake of Death

The Daughter

Four

Also available

Invisible

The Dead of Winter

Fractured

Krampus

The Blood Runs Darker

Christmas

Whispers

Tailgate

Download: Author.to/bmb

Thank You

Thank you for your incredible patience. It's been 18 months since my last release and the words of support have pushed me through a little case of writer's block. This book has been in the works for much longer, having started out as a novella of a very different body. Now, incredibly, exists three different versions, this one being the final draft.

I would like to thank the many of you who continue to read and explore the stories. It means the absolute world to me. I look forward to continuing on this ever-changing and exciting journey and hope that you stay on the path with me.

All my love and best wishes.

xBilly

PROLOGUE

The Third Day

He stood at the mouth of the bridge and stared down. A crimson blot sailed into the black stream and diluted until there was nothing left to see. The sky remained stark, a hallmark of late summer as daylight married dusk.

A spark flickered, a momentary glow as the threat of flames loomed. The silent calm after the throttling storm was unsettling but more unsettling was the realisation that someone so mammoth in his mind could be so little and worthless.

It took a moment for his thoughts to stop spiraling and then he knew. He couldn't fix this. The damage was already done. The only thing he could do was finish it and move on with his life.

So, watching his victim groan as blood washed his face, the man reached down and lifted a rock. He brought it up, wondering momentarily what it might feel like to crush the bones in someone's head. He would soon know.

He rested his free hand on the edge of the toppled car, now just a broken shell in a rambling heap, and moved closer. Once he was only an inch from the injured man's face, he simply whispered, 'This one's for my sister.'

One crack to the side of the head and he waited for life to disappear from his victim's eyes.

CHAPTER ONE

Chris

He arrived under the cover of darkness. Dusk had already meddled with the brash sunset, the late summer evenings now transitioning into an autumnal cool. Chris Burns stepped out of his car, parked beneath the viaduct at the back of the modest cottages that acted as guards to the cascaded wealthier houses on the upper crests. He carried a bag, a vital possession that held everything he needed as he crept along the back pathway of the dark, empty house that would be his home for the next several days.

The back walls hadn't changed much. The rusty lock clinked open as he listened for life, looking round into the next gardens. Nothing much changed in the entire place. Walter Prentice's sinister army of glowering gnomes still stood guard, and on the other side, Karen Barton's Garden resembled an unruly woodland. There was just enough cover on both sides that he hoped not to be seen.

Chris hurried inside, slammed the door shut, and took a quick glance through the small oval window. Satisfied that his car was anonymous enough to escape suspicion, he felt a flicker of relief. Nobody was out there observing his movements.

As he flicked the light switch, a flat sheet of dust along his eyeline and drapes of cobwebs in the kitchen corners stunned him. The once-immaculate kitchen lay stagnant, now a testament to neglect. The memory of its former state died instantly as he confronted this new scattered reality. At least there was light.

Chris set about making himself coffee, knowing it would be his faithful companion for the next few days. Sleep would be a luxury he couldn't afford until his task was complete. He had a proper electric pot in the car, but that could wait until tomorrow. Right now, he just wanted to begin. Three years of painstaking research had led him to this moment, where he could finally unveil his masterpiece. Everything was in place.

With a small bag in one hand and a steaming

mug in the other, Chris climbed the stairs. In a dusty mirror on the upper landing, he caught a glimpse of himself. At thirty-seven years of age, he had found his inner hipster. His beard, a mass of auburn strands, curled into each other until they reached a sharp point amid his honed pecks. His oval emerald eyes, framed by long black lashes, commanded attention, disguising the faint lines that had started to etch themselves at the corners. He had yet to be marred by bitterness or the lust for blood that he knew would come. For now, he wore his charm like a coat of arms, capable of switching it on even in the obscenest of circumstances.

Pulling down the ladder, he stared up into the loft, a place that had once been a haven for his imagination while the rest of the house resembled a dental surgery. Now, there was no one to frantically scrub away the daily grime or chase away the nocturnal webs that housed the spindly legs of frantic creatures.

Climbing up, he carefully placed the mug on a wooden beam inside the loft. He slid the bag to a safe distance, ensuring that his entrance wouldn't cause any accidental spills. Leaning down, he hit the nearby light switch, plunging the house back into the darkness it wore so cordially now. Once inside the loft, he pulled up the ladder and closed the hatch.

It took him a moment to balance himself. He stood upon the flattened creaky wooden ladder, engulfed by the faint scent of aged timber and unforgotten memories. The light in there was dim, enhanced by a small amount of light seeping in through gaps in the old, weathered roof tiles. Cobwebs stretched like veils across the corners, their silken threads catching on the occasional glint of light. Cardboard boxes, stacked haphazardly, bore witness to the remnants of the lives left behind.

As he switched on his laptop, a small layer of light bathed the surroundings, providing a semblance of comfort in this old forgotten landscape. It was the same device that had served as his repository of gathered intel, and in this environment, it provided a sense of familiarity. Chris hadn't anticipated feeling this way, but the emotions that washed over him were a mix of nostalgia and determination. He had explored every nook and cranny of this house, memorising every lyrical carving across the pitched walls towering over the eaves.

In the background, a cricket burred, offering a subtle companion to his solitary task. It was a lonely undertaking, but a necessary one. He tapped quickly on the keys, sipping from the warm mug, and then waited with unyielding patience as a secret cloud unfurled at the right corner of his screen. Every pocket of data lay encrypted within, ready to birth his miniature Armageddon upon those who had wronged him.

Plugging in his phone, he hoped that the hotspot connection had improved since his last visit. Another sip from the mug sent the black coffee burning at the back of his throat. He reached into the bag, feeling for something less technical as the screen exploded with colour.

Chris's thoughts drifted to the journey that had brought him here, not just the twelve hours on the road retracing a well-worn path into the past. The three years of tenacious research had been arduous, yet mostly worth it. While it wasn't everything he needed, it had provided the foundation for his mission. Cleaning the tarnished reputation that had been unjustly thrust upon him was no easy task, but he had uncovered muck on those who presented themselves as saints. The vacant space behind his eyes proved that. The tempered, untraceable invasion into their lives hadn't been as easy as he once hoped, but it hadn't been impossible either.

He carried the binoculars in his hands as his feet crunched on the partially floored surface beneath him. Reaching the pitched window, he wiped away the family of spiders who had inhabited this space undisturbed for far too long. One spider landed on his skin, but it didn't faze him. He trusted the unknown more than he trusted any single human he had ever met. The little spider scurried across the inked python on his right arm, a tickle on the bronzed hairs that permanently resided there. With both hands cradling the binoculars against his eyes, he focused his gaze.

It took a moment to locate the house. The trees

had continued to grow and live, marking the passage of time. Still, he found it relatively quickly. His reasons for observing the house had changed. There was no one at the end of the phone, nobody smiling from the upstairs window. Only cold, immersing hatred remained as he watched a family, now reduced in numbers, enjoy the last drops of wine as they concluded their family barbecue.

Slowly, he turned his attention to the screen behind him, now completely fired up and ready for action. The day he had long awaited had finally arrived, the day when they would pay for their deeds. He wondered if the people in this village ever thought of him. Soon, they would think of nothing but him. And when those hours and minutes came, he would scorch their lives to the ground.

CHAPTER TWO

Sleep was necessary but inconsequential. Chris had never slept through a full night in twenty years. Not since that fateful night when everything changed. He had dreamed often, exploring his way through murky worlds that were only vaguely reminiscent of the one he knew. Still, there were times when he relished the unknown because it was an upgrade on what had remained of his reality after the natives picked over the bones of his life.

Being back here was more painful than Chris could have ever imagined. He wasn't a sentimental man. It wasn't a luxury he had ever afforded himself. Not when the things and the people he might get sentimental over had betrayed him. Still, there was this house. A tomb where he could hide and feel relatively safe.

A sliver of light broke through the window and Chris wondered if he should unpack the car before his neighbours began their day. He tapped on the laptop and brought the screen to life. He had planned with precision but the one thing he hadn't decided upon was the order of how he would unleash his revenge. This village was a house of dominoes waiting to collapse. Once the first one came down, it wouldn't be long before carnage ensued.

He lit a cigarette, a habit he'd fought against many times but that now served as a constant companion he didn't really want. A bit like the tattooed serpents on his skin. The silver smoke rose instantly, forming a helmet round his head as he stared towards the trees that lined the backward ridge.

Then, he took to the screen again. It was time to scratch the itch, fire off the first bullet and watch the first one tumble. He flicked away the ash, watching as it fell on the floor and let a sardonic smile carve his face. He opened the video file just so he knew it was the correct one. It wasn't a reel he was particularly keen to watch again. It had been ugly enough the first time, but he certainly couldn't afford to get this wrong.

It only took a moment for Chris to know he was on the right clip as he sat back in the old wooden chair and took another deep drag. He had already lined up the firewall, encrypted the file so securely that even the top brass in MI5 would be unlikely to access it. He had already prepped it so that the video would go to its rightful destination first. It would then bounce across the rest of the target list.

Chris thought of the other person who had once resided in this house. Long gone, but never forgotten. Forgiveness didn't come easily. He could still see her frail pointed face, pinched lips pressed down in anxiety as she urged him never to come near this village again. He had complied for twenty years, bearing the brunt of the pitchfork crew as they sought someone, anyone to blame.

He hit the send button, a momentary satisfaction that he could not have foreseen. The first step to retribution he believed he was owed.

Rising from the seat, he felt a powerful surge in his body as if someone had injected a bolt of lightning into it.

Time ticked. He had no concept of it. Dawn had arrived but it could be five o'clock at night for all he knew or cared. All he knew was that soon, someone's life would be in ruins. Not the ruins they'd left him in because Chris was tough. There was a certain resilience to children who grew up fatherless and with stern mothers who rarely expressed love. He wondered if the precious figureheads of the soulless village would be so resilient. He doubted it. They had shrouded each other for long enough. Once the little unimportant people learned that those who lived in the ivory towers were so heinous, Chris hoped it would be the nail in the coffin that was needed. Once these shallow minded morons were forced to face the insidious underlayer of their own community,

'Don't get ahead of yourself,' he whispered, looking at the screen once more. He stumped the cigarette butt out on the hard wooden floor and rested his back. He closed his eyes and quashed the excitement because the damage hadn't been done yet. It might be hours before Max McDermott opened the video. By then, it might have gone semi-viral. It was all it would take to destroy the man who had once helped destroy him. Chris's only regret was that he wouldn't see the look on Max's face when justice was finally served.

CHAPTER THREE

Max McDermott sat at the head of the table in the board room and flicked his pen. At sixty, he was on the eve of retirement and could not wait to take his wife on the trip to Egypt he'd been promising for five years. The day had been uneventful so far, filled with the mundane tasks that came with being head of a law firm.

He looked at the screen in front of him, glad of the peace and quiet and noticed a box spinning from wall to wall. It displayed a notification that invited him to open. He wondered if he should quickly report it to IT and then close it down. After all, companies like this were always getting hit by spyware. However, there was something persistent about the way it flickered on the screen, almost like it was hypnotising him to open it up.

Anyway, Max was naturally inquisitive, so he discarded what little doubt nagged at him and clicked on the box. The screen became animated with a mixture of vibrant colours and a timer that quickly climbed towards the finale of one hundred percent.

As the emails unfolded before him, Max's heart began to race. He rose from the chair, looked around him because he feared someone else might have received the same collection of emails. Worse still, it might have been someone in this office who sent it in the first place. There was one person who might have been guilty, but he wasn't sure they would have the sophistication to deliver blackmail this way. Besides, he had already paid that due.

His phone rang then. His wife Rainie was calling him. Just as she did every time she thought of something else to add to their planned trip. He wasn't sure he could speak to her now because his throat had dried, he suspected his voice would croak and she always knew when he was stressed. Once again, this dark lie had come back to haunt him. One mistake and it was following him into retirement.

'Hello, love. Everything alright?'

Silence.

'Rainie, love. Are you there?' He heard sniffing, like she was blowing her nose. It rose to audible sobbing but there were no words to follow. 'Rainie, you're scaring me. What's happened?'

'I've seen it. You dirty pig. I've saw what you did.'

'I'm coming home.'

Her voice rose then, deepening in anger. 'Yes, you are. To get your filthy clothes and anything else that belongs to you out of my house. I'm calling a locksmith right now.'

'Rainie, it's not true. It's been doctored. I promise you.'

She snorted then. 'What do you take me for? I know you think I'm just a stupid woman who relies on you to support me but give me some credit. You think I don't recognise my own husband's body.'

He knew he couldn't talk his way out of this. Someone had meticulously put together everything from the moment he stepped into that facility right through to the payments he'd made to keep it hush. After all, he'd have lost his practice, his life, everything he'd built for the last forty years. 'It was once. Just one time. It was during that bad period where you moved into the spare room.'

'Oh, shut up. I would have thought making such a poor excuse for what you've done might have been beneath you but in the end, you're just a penis on two legs. I shouldn't have expected anything better.'

'Please don't do anything hasty. Remember we fly out next week.'

She let out laughter then, a riotous cutting laugh that merged with her sobs. 'Yes, I am flying next week. Alone.'

There was a pause then, a momentary reprieve from the emotional inclines that had dominated the call.

'How old is she?'

'What?'

'You heard me, Max. How old is the girl in that video. I mean, there must be a reason you've paid two lots of fifty thousand pounds from our life savings to a perfect stranger. That must be the most expensive prostitute you've hired.'

'She wasn't a prostitute,' he said, meekly. The front of his head aching with the realisation that if this was sent to both him and his wife, it might well have gone elsewhere. He let out a deep gasp and clutched his beating chest.

'No, she wasn't,' said Rainie, her voice finally settling. 'She was a child and you bloody raped her.'

*

A welcome light filtered through the windows, casting a gentle glow on the worn wooden steps as Chris made his way down from the loft. Each creak of the staircase echoed through the quiet house, disrupting the peaceful stillness that had settled overnight.

As Chris descended, his gaze unintentionally fell upon the pictures adorning the walls, memories carefully captured in time. Each step seemed to correspond with a different stage of his life, a visual reminder of the passage of time he had tried so hard to ignore.

The first picture, a faded photograph of a beaming young boy with messy hair and a toothy grin, greeted Chris as he took the initial step. It depicted a time of innocence and simplicity, a world untainted by the burdens that now weighed heavily on his shoulders. He could almost hear the carefree laughter that once filled the air.

With each subsequent step, the pictures unfolded a narrative of his journey. A teenage Chris, awkward and unsure, stood frozen in a moment captured on the second step. He'd felt so self-assured then but now he could see the anxiety and self-doubt in his unmoving eyes.

Moving down further, the photographs chronicled the milestones of adulthood. A graduation photo displayed a proud Chris, his eyes sparkling with ambition and dreams of a promising future. A promising future that had been stolen from him. The compromises of reality didn't feature on the wall because the face of abandonment didn't come armed with pride.

His foot reached the fifth step, and a photograph captured a moment of deep joy and genuine love. It was a picture of Chris and his late mother, Cathy, arms wrapped around each other in a warm embrace. It should have been a joyous memory. It wasn't. It was a stark reminder of the abandonment, the betrayal and most cruelly, the curve in the road where he had been left completely alone. Unconditional love had ceased to exist. There was only accusation then.

His footsteps grew heavier as he reached the ground floor. It's not that he had never seen his mother again. There had been visits. None to this house, though. No opportunity to be placed back in the bosom of his childhood home. He'd simply ceased to be here, either forgotten or berated and labelled a killer.

Finally, Chris reached the ground floor, his journey down memory lane complete. He stood at the foot of the staircase, taking a moment to reciprocate the hatred that had been mounted on him. It should have been hard to find it because Chris had never been a hateful person. He was going to be a doctor. That was his ambition but life being what it was, he'd gone into computer forensics instead. Now, it was a sideward step rather than a retreat. He loved his work and it had afforded him the opportunity to return to the village. To unleash some well-deserved karma.

He passed the lounge, unwilling to visit there yet. That would be a painful reminder too far. It's where Cathy existed. Not just then, but now, her ghostly presence as silent and stern as she ever was. He wasn't ready. He would avoid tearful recrimination because in the end, Cathy had been as much a victim as he was. He moved to the kitchen, sunlight painting the room with a gentle warmth. He hit the button on the kettle and allowed a moment of satisfaction to engulf him. Max McDermott had been instrumental in his destruction. It seemed only fitting that he should feel the wrath first.

Chris poured himself a coffee and moved to the back door. He had a morning cigarette with the door barely ajar. If he listened hard enough, he was sure he would hear the tittle tattle of those old familiar voices over the singing tweet of birds. Would they be talking about Max yet? Would the video have spread yet? Even if they didn't watch it, they would learn about it and that would be satisfying enough. The destruction probably hadn't begun yet, but that was none of Chris's business. He had already moved on.

CHAPTER FOUR

It started like a lesion, a tiny grain of black that festered and grew. Slowly, unforgivingly, it gripped Connie with its insidious wrath, weighing heavier on her shoulders with each passing day. It felt like an endless, suffocating darkness that consumed her from deep within.

Connie Gibbs couldn't remember life before her first-born daughter, Lara. She had the faintest memory of growing up, the middle of three sisters, always feeling inadequate sandwiched between the beautiful elder one and the smart, eccentric youngest. So, she had to forge her own identity, which she did by marrying Richie and raising three kids of whom she was immensely proud.

The youngest of Connie's sisters died years ago. The postmortem revealed an undetected birth defect in her heart, causing a great deal of anguish for the rest of the family. Marcia had been the closest thing to a live wire the family had produced. She had been effervescent for the short twenty-seven years she graced the earth. That loss had weighed heavily on Connie, but she had to carry on because, by then, she had already married Richie and given birth to her three kids.

Shortly afterward, Connie's mother passed away, and then a year later, her father. She had grieved for them, but not as intensely as she had grieved for Marcia. She didn't think she would ever experience loss like that again or know pain so achingly raw and unrelenting. Until Lara.

It was possible for Connie to count her blissfully happy moments on less than two hands. She had been so consumed by her grief that those moments seemed to pale in comparison. After all, how could she enjoy the memory of her daughter's birth without feeling cheated of her in death? How could she celebrate her boys without feeling the constant absence of Lara, a third of that puzzle missing? Yet, she wouldn't be without the grief now. If she couldn't have Lara, this was the poor but necessary substitute.

Connie emerged from her deep thoughts when the chimes on the shop door jangled, signaling the arrival of the ladies. Saved by the bell.

'I don't know about you, but I could murder a cup of vodka,' Winnie exclaimed.

Connie chuckled as Winnie crossed the floor. 'How are you, Win? Good to see you, love.'

'I almost didn't make it. Honest to God, that husband of mine will send me over the edge. Do you know he told me he was considering leaving me for someone else?'

Reaching for the coffee maker, Connie began to laugh, finding it the perfect tonic. 'How is he?'

'Oh, good days and bad days. Yesterday, he remembered I was his wife and that he used to be a gardener, so I got a peck on the lips and my weeding done. Today, he's asking if I heard the news about the Kennedy assassination and looking at me like I'm the hierarchy of Salem.'

Connie chuckled a little harder, feeling grateful that her oldest friend had made it to the group this week. She wondered how someone could go through such a devastating thing every day and still be so full of life. In fact, she might have envied it if she allowed herself to escape her own self-indulgence. 'Oh, should we have wine at this afternoon's group?'

'I'm amazed you have to ask,' the woman replied curtly. 'You don't have to ask me twice if I want a glass of Pinot. Should I nip over to the pub and grab a bottle?'

Connie glanced outwards, then remembered she had already tucked three bottles into the fridge a few weeks before. 'No need, unless forty people turn up, which I doubt. I've got a few bottles in the chill out the back. Can you grab me the box of flowers in the far corner? I put them aside for this afternoon.'

She disappeared into the back, reminding herself that she had also set aside some petunias for Lara. She would go over later, give Lara the flowers, and have a chat. That always settled her a little. 'Did you hear about Phil and Melanie splitting up? Apparently, someone found out he was having an affair and sent her an anonymous picture of Phil at some event with his mistress.'

'That's cruel. He must have upset someone,' laughed Winnie. 'Oh, here comes the girls. Better get the coffee machine on just in case Sal is still pretending to be tea total.'

'Give her what she wants, just as long as she's brought some cakes from her bakery.' Connie leaned into the fridge, grabbed the first bottle and a few wine glasses from the sideboard.

Moving back to the centre of the shop, her friends gathered around the central island, already pulling at the stems in the box.

Winnie spoke more vivaciously than the other ladies, her loud Hebridean accent making her sound more like a farmer's wife than a dental nurse. 'I propose a toast to the success of the shop. Let's get this place on the social media map.' She held up her phone, moved towards Connie, and snapped a picture of the gathering.

Connie suddenly frowned. 'Is Rainie not joining us today? I haven't seen her in too long.'

'No, darling. She didn't answer the phone,' replied Sal.

No one was overly concerned about Rainie's absence since she rarely showed up to anything these days.

Uproarious laughter filled the room for the next hour until the crowd began to disperse. Once alone, Connie decided she would close early. She felt slightly tipsy, which was nothing new since she spent most of her days just keeping herself apace. For twenty years, it had become her customary way of getting through the day and, sometimes, the night.

If Winnie knew just what it took for Connie to get out of bed, putting one foot in front of the other, she might not have been so keen on the idea of a wine afternoon. Still, that was Connie's cross to bear. If she wouldn't share it with her husband, she certainly wouldn't share it with anyone else.

*

The loft was shrouded in a haze of smoke, tendrils dancing in the dim light as Chris sat back at his cluttered desk. His laptop screen glowed softly, illuminating the room with a pale blue hue. With a heavy sigh, he brought his fingers to the keyboard, preparing the next file.

As Chris tapped on the keys, his heart raced with

a touch of trepidation. The cursor hovered over the folder, a complex collection of evidence against someone who had once stood at the centre of their very own Camelot. The sword had been drawn then. Twenty years later it would fall on the head of Darren Philips, and he wouldn't even see it coming.

His gaze settled on a picture of Lara, his childhood sweetheart, whose absence may well have been the catalyst for the growing hatred in him. Lara was dead. She had drowned in the lake of the village, poised for a wonderful life that had been cruelly snatched on the eve of his very own downfall. The whispered promises had dissipated in less than a fraction of a heartbeat. Not the image of her radiant smile or those sparkling eyes, nor the essence of a love that he knew transcended time could give that back to him. Their youthful exuberance had been quashed; stolen kisses muted as their shared dream had simply ended.

In that smoky loft, the weight of his memories pressed against his chest, the continued silence of his life consuming him. He tapped a finger on Lara's image and let the ache surge into him. Sometimes he spoke to her. Today he didn't feel like speaking. So, he opened a blank page on the screen and began to type.

As the words flowed from his fingertips, Chris's emotions spilled onto the screen. He confessed how her absence had shaped his life, how the pain of losing her had propelled him into the urge for success then the relentless pursuit of revenge. His soul poured onto that page; the tormented nights re-captured as unspoken words remained unsaid.

'I'm doing it all for you,' he typed, his fingers trembling with vulnerability. Each keystroke felt like a release, though there was more to it than that. Every person he took down for their part in punishing him for something he hadn't done added to the freedom. His only regret was that they wouldn't know where it had come from. Revenge was only part of it. Knowing the impact on their lives would be equally satisfying.

He copied the contents of the page and put it into an email. One day he would find it again. Right now, it would disappear into some online vessel only he could access. A tap of the enter key and the message flew through cyberspace, words whispered into the digital abyss. He closed the screen, deciding on a break and stared into the smoke-filled air.

Now he knew the longing for Lara would never end. The ardent quest for revenge wouldn't change that. Smoke curled round him as he tugged on the growing beard on his face. He wouldn't stop now. That quest wasn't solely about Lara, nor Cathy, nor even about himself. There were people in this village who existed outside the periphery of decency whilst hiding in the confines of their pretentious armour and he was determined he would bring them out into daylight. He knew neither Lara, the most beautiful soul he'd ever known, nor his mother, a woman who was almost the right-hand woman of God, would approve. It wasn't about their approval now. One day he would honour the dreams he and Lara had spoken of, their shared desires that would only ever be a tribute and never the sprawling expanse of a fulfilled life together.

He crossed the creaky floor, navigating the wooden beams before heading downstairs and kept his closed laptop at his side. He needed to get out of here for a while because he was starting to feel just a little too claustrophobic up here. He had somewhere he needed to be anyway. The pendulum was already swinging for Darren Phillips. He may already know about Max's fall from grace. What he didn't know yet was that he would soon be in the frame for orchestrating it.

CHAPTER FIVE

Fleeting decisions made in haste rarely served anyone. Usually, though, those very decisions cannot be reversed. Max McDermott sat in his car, his shattered life beating slowly and painful to its conclusion as he found himself on the slip road leaving the M8. The world around him seemed to fade into the background as he contemplated the unthinkable.

His mind swirled with a tempest of emotions, each one tearing at his sanity and pushing him closer to the edge. The revelations in those emails had left him exposed and he wondered how many people had received it by now.

Max stepped out of the car, his legs trembling beneath him. The cold metal of the fence pressed against his hands as he climbed up, his heart pounding in his chest. Everything seemed to blur in the cold blue daylight. The only thought in his mind now was that he couldn't go home, he couldn't take the look of disgust that would be in his wife's expression nor the damage it would do to his relationship with his kids and grandkids.

No, there was only one way out.

He climbed up and perched precariously on the fence, the wind biting at his skin. Every vehicle passing under the bridge sounded like the whoosh of water in a feral river. He cried, though he didn't know who for. How could someone do this to him? He didn't know the girl was fifteen. He was as much a victim as she was. People wouldn't understand that though. They'd label him a pedophile and throw him to the wolves when really his only wrongdoing had been infidelity.

He eyed his car, abandoned on the side of the road, and tried to reason with himself. Perhaps people would understand, maybe they would see that he'd been punished enough. After all, half his life savings had been paid to someone to stop this from ever coming out. It seems that blackmailers weren't to be trusted. Who knew?

A surge that felt like a shock bore through hm and he began to count backwards. If he was going to do this, he had to do it quickly. As he approached the end of the countdown, he put one foot out so that it hovered above the passing traffic. A gust of wind was enough to make the decision for him and as he opened his eyes, Max listened to the scream of a ten-wheeler truck trying to swerve and halt. Maybe in the few brief seconds before death, he might have regretted his decision. By then, it was simply too late.

*

The engine of Chris's car hummed softly as he parked outside the Gibbs family home. The familiar sight of the house brought an unexpected ache to the surface and his hands gripped the steering wheel. It was difficult to reconcile the memories and the intertwining hatred.

His gaze fixated on the figure emerging from the front door. Richie Gibbs, Lara's father, stepped out, his presence commanding attention even from a distance. His physique, sculpted by long hours outdoors, still displayed the strength and resilience that had once made Connie the envy of local society. Not that she minded, he recalled.

Chris continued to watch, raging. It was difficult to equate the feelings of insurmountable hatred with the man he knew he now was. There had just been this urge. Ever since his mother's death, there had been this incurable desire to face off with the people of Crianlarich. He just didn't expect in the beginning that it would become a reality.

Chris didn't think of Lara too long. In the beginning it had been too painful. Now, it was because no matter how passionate she could be, she would not approve of this. This was her family, and he was out to cause damage. It hurt him almost as much as it would hurt them but he needed to do this so he could finally put closure to everything that had happened.

His mind wandered back to a time when Richie had been a pillar of support in his life. After losing his own father at a young age, Chris had found solace in the warmth of the Gibbs household. Richie had taken him under his wing, teaching him about horses and, honestly, life in general. Knowing all of that only tainted the memory further. If there was ever any doubt in Chris's mind, there was always something to remind him why he was doing this.

Chris's fists clenched. He wanted to storm that house, vent his inner turmoil, and let them know the damage they'd done. Could they even know? Did they remember? It was hard to imagine not but maybe he was insignificant to them. Now, that really would hurt.

As Richie drew closer, his dark Celtic features etched with sorrow and loss, Chris felt the wave of guilt that he knew would eventually come. This man before him had shown him such kindness, treated him like a son even though he had his own sons to contend with at the time. Chris wanted to stamp his fists on the dashboard. Why was he so conflicted when he'd been so sure before arriving? Now, in the midst of their lives, humanity re-instigated, he felt stupid for not considering that he would feel something.

Still, there was no two people more instrumental in destroying his life and, subsequently, his mother's. Richie and Connie would take what they had doled out. Even if it eventually consumed him.

Chris dared not think of his life now. He knew better than to sour it with these strands of vengeance.

He watched Richie approach a black Mondeo and released his grip on the steering wheel. He looked out of his window, downwards, so his eyes connected with a rocky path on the other side of the road. The rocky path well-travelled, he thought. He wanted to honour Lara but more importantly, he wanted to honour his mother because she had been driven to her death, suffering the loss of her own son from her life but also cruelly treated like a lepper for too long. He hoped that from the abyss of death Lara could forgive him. After all, he was only paying back those who had labelled him a cold-blooded killer.

CHAPTER SIX

Pricking her finger on a thorn, Connie gasped. She muttered to herself and then trimmed once more on the stem of the orchid. The flower wasn't native to these parts and were hard to source at times, but she loved them and decided these would be perfect for Lara's grave.

Connie regretted that it was the only gift she could give her daughter, who would be celebrating her thirty seventh birthday next week. Thirty-seven years since Connie had given birth to the greatest gift God had granted her. Then, taken from her a mere seventeen years later. The anniversary of Lara's death was also imminent. That wasn't a thought for now.

The door opened.

'I'll be with you in a minute,' she said, her back to the door.

The man walked in and pressed his hands on the counter.

Connie lowered her scissors and turned.

'Hi, I wanted to buy some flowers for my

beautiful wife, but I couldn't find anywhere else to buy them.'

She laughed heartily, her eyes filling. 'You old rocket. You don't need to buy me flowers. Not when you could treat me to three courses at McGonigle's and a seven-day all-inclusive to Majorca.'

'Seven days, huh? Cheap date. I was thinking three-week cruise round the Caribbean but, I'm only the husband.' He reached into his pocket and took a blue paper wallet out. Instantly, the cover of the packet revealed golden beaches, towering cliffs that soared into the sky and aqua waters. Like Crianlarich, if Scotland wasn't so grey and miserable most of the time.

Connie flushed with guilt then. She had pre-empted his lovely gesture with words that almost sounded ungrateful. How was she to know though? That wasn't her real guilt. The real internal battle existed within Connie because she knew she had a wonderful husband and two lovely sons, but they never felt enough. They were the sharp points of a Bermuda triangle where everything else had been sucked into the uncompromising abyss.

'I was going to suggest the Winterville for dinner tonight, but Drew has invited himself to another barbecue. Apparently, nobody barbecues the steaks like his old mum. Even though I keep telling him that it is me who does the cooking.'

'Hey,' she said, good-humouredly slapping him on the arm. 'I do the marinade.'

'And it's fantastic. Are you closing up now?'

'No,' she lied. She wanted to get to the cemetery without Richie knowing. He went over there on birthdays and anniversaries but had once protested over the amount of time she used to spend there. Now, she went in secret, and she'd come to like it that way.

'Will you stop off at the butchers on the way home. I have to go up and muck out the stable. I will be back in a couple of hours.'

Connie swallowed her sigh of relief. She sensed he wanted her to go up and help at the stable, but she hated going there. It was just another reminder and one she didn't need.

'Right, I'm going,' he said, rolling his eyes.

She moved round the counter, grabbed his right buttock, and helped him out the door. She turned to the mirror and took a deep hard look at herself. 'Not long to the big six-oh now,' she muttered, toying with the waves in her dyed blonde hair. She could see the lines that tightened her once sparkling green eyes. Everything drooped now, her jowls, the once full cheekbones and even the lobes of her ears. Some might say she was an attractive, natural fifty-something. She just felt dowdy and worn. Not even Richie's relentless enthusiasm for her would convince her otherwise. In fact, the only time she felt at ease in herself was when she was blind plastered drunk. These days, that wasn't often enough.

*

From his secluded vantage point, Chris watched as Richie Gibbs stood in Connie's shop and disappeared inside. The bitterness that had taken root within him intensified, fueled by the knowledge that Connie had played a significant role in orchestrating the hatred that branded him a killer. His gaze lingered on the shop's entrance, loathing festering beneath him and he toyed with the idea, ridiculously, of storming over there and telling them what they'd done.

But as his eyes shifted away from the shop, they landed on his mother's house, weathered, and worn from the outside, a reflection of how he felt about this place. The shabby house, dilapidated on the surface but a little less so on the inside, served as a manifestation of his physical pain. The heartbreak that had fueled this vendetta lay within the brickwork of those walls, wedged in every crevice of the floors, porous from every stick of furniture.

Chris turned once more, now staring down onto the pier that led to the lake. It was there that it had all truly fallen apart. He closed his eyes and for the briefest moment he was transferred back to that time. Lara's lifeless body lay on the pier.

The memory flooded his mind, unwelcome yet relentless. The sight of her limp body and the overwhelming sense of helplessness washed over him anew. In that defining moment, he cradled Lara in his arms, her death proving to be that moment that would be the catalyst for every decision he would make. The other moment that defined the next twenty years was the arrival of his mother, Cathy, who arrived first, witnessing the devastation etched across his face.

Cathy's head had been turned though. The lies that followed not only broke him but destroyed the once unbreakable bond between him and his mother. The recollection tightened its grip on Chris's heart, the devastation of betrayal had cut deep, and he was left with another devastating moment in his life. One that he himself might have been able to avoid if only he had been willing to forgive. Tears formed though he fought them back before they fell.

Through blurred vision, Chris contemplated the pain the Gibbs family had been through. In different circumstances their pain might have been interconnected but they had severed that. His hatred had become a double-edged sword. Even with tears forming a brief film over his eyes, he had clarity. There would be no healing without retribution, no normality without justice.

With a deep breath, Chris wiped away his tears

and allowed himself a moment of respite. One day he hoped he would be free of the anguish, to think of Lara without hurting, to recall his mother without feeling the weight of her betrayal or the guilt of her death.

The echoes of grief subsided. He turned back to look at the house knowing that would soon be gone. A sale sign would soon go up and the village would know that he had unshackled himself from this sorry little place. Not before he made sure they knew he had been here and that those who had scorned him, banishing him in fact, had finally paid the price.

CHAPTER SEVEN

Detective Inspector Ryan Starling leaned against the window of his home office, the view both spectacular and dull at the very same time. It was a rugged landscape, starkly contrasting with the fast-paced urban environment he was so used to. He ran a hand through his cropped dark hair, his sharp jawline a taut reflection of the determined man he was. Even with the intention of working from home today, Ryan still dressed in a sharp suit and tie, exuding an air of professionalism, every inch the seasoned detective.

On the phone with his boss, Ryan's voice carried the echoes of his Scottish roots, though there was a strange mid-Atlantic twang there that made people assume he wasn't born and bred here. He was. His mother was Aberdonian, his father a miner from the East end of Glasgow who had now retired to an upstairs villa in Palma Nova.

Ryan rarely smiled, rarely got in-jokes, and had become the pariah of his former team due to his formality and lack of willingness to shout for a round.

He never moved beyond the task at hand which had made him unpopular. So much so that the Chief of police at MIT had orchestrated a promoted secondment for him. A favour to everyone, he'd joked.

'It's not a punishment,' drawled Pat McKinlay, once again explaining to Ryan what he'd said several times. 'Bluntly speaking, Ry, your social skills are lacking. It's why you're such a bloody good detective because you don't seem to feel for anyone. However, it doesn't work in a team where you have to have each other's backs. I need you to take this time to work on how you interact with people. It's the perfect place to do it. The crime rate is low, almost non-existent within the village itself. That allows time for you to get to know people with your police work on the back burner and then we'll get you home again.'

Ryan couldn't hide his dissatisfaction. It was deader than a do-do here. If a drunk person raised their voice at closing time, the entire village talked about how someone had turned violent at the pub last night 'I understand,' said Ryan. 'It seems I am too candid for some people but that's alright because I am here to do a job.'

A sigh from the other end of the phone didn't deter Ryan in his belief, nor did it incur a reaction. He knew it reflected someone's frustration though he didn't understand why McKinley was frustrated because he hadn't been relegated to Hell's own paradise for a six-month assignment that barely existed.

Pat, a normally patient man, blew into the receiver once more. 'Ryan, son. I'll repeat it's not a punishment. You'll do well to remember that. You'll be glad of the experience when you come back and show this bloody lot that you're as loyal to your colleagues as the next man.'

Ryan didn't understand it. Loyal in what way? He'd never reported any of his colleagues and challenged those who made mistakes head-on. He had once brought donuts after someone accused him of eating the last one and not replenishing them. Not long ago, he contributed quite a handsome sum to the retirement pot of a man who had been most kind to him when others would snicker and snort at his expense. Ryan had no feelings for those people, but he did find it odd that they mistook his lack of social interaction for stupidity.

His grey eyes narrowed; his slim lips pursed as he rubbed his finger along his bony pointed nose. What was so important about interpersonal skills anyway? He wasn't rude to people. He asked the right questions in interrogations and always treated the perpetrators like human beings. Not all of his colleagues were blessed in that way.

'I wanted to ask you, Ryan. Have you come across Max McDermott yet?'

'No, I've heard the name,' said Ryan.

'We received a very disturbing video clip. It came in an anonymous email.'

'Encrypted, most likely,' said Ryan, continuing to stare at that beautiful vast and very unbusy landscape.

'Yes, indeed,' continued Pat. 'It is being investigated by tech now, but I've heard rumours about its content already and I'm not liking it. I just wondered if you had heard anything?'

'No, not a dickie,' he said, mirroring words he'd seen in a detective show a while ago but realising Pat didn't find it funny when there was no laughter on the line.

'Okay, well, keep your ear to the ground. It might not come to anything, but he lives at the top of the village up there and I'm just hoping that we don't have any trouble.'

'Would you like me to go and speak to him?'

Pat went silent for a moment. 'No need. Unfortunately, Mr. McDermott died a few hours ago. Threw himself off a bridge. Messy, and inconvenient for our guys in that part of the world but it's all done and dusted now.'

The call ended and Ryan found himself wondering exactly what might have been the content of the video. What would drive a person to killing themselves? He made a mental note to ask a few questions without drawing attention to himself. He wasn't a nosy man, but he was inherently curious because without it, he feared he wouldn't be much of a detective.

Straightening his suit and adjusting his tie, Ryan decided to immerse himself in what was happening in the village because he suspected that, beneath the appearance of serenity, even this idyllic place masked a certain darkness.

*

Chris trailed Richie Gibbs from a distance, his eyes fixated on the scene before him. Richie's car came to a stop, and Chris caught his breath as he witnessed Ellie, Lara's best friend, standing at the window, taking Richie's hand. He had spent months seeking out scandal and found nothing. Was it possible they were a family at ease with lying and cheating? He hoped so.

It was unexpected. Ellie had been Lara's best friend their entire lives, as short a time as that transpired to be. Chris hadn't really factored Ellie, or her husband, Tommy, into things. They were, after all, his best friends too. Chris could only imagine that they were the two people who might have spoken up for him though he had cut ties with them as quickly as he'd cut ties with his own mother.

The narrative he had constructed in his own head fueled his quest for revenge. It was something he had mulled over for the best part of seventeen years. Then, finally, one day, he used his own resources to dally down the dark path. He'd left no stone unturned once he began to delve into the lives of those who he now vowed to take vengeance on, but it would never have occurred to him that anything would happen between Ellie and Richie. He was old enough to be her father.

The questions tumbled; the answers lay dormant. There were things he now suspected he had missed. It was the pitfalls of doing his investigation from a distance. Was Ellie having an affair with Richie? Did anyone else know about it? Doubt gnawed and he found himself in the realms of uncertainty. After all, he did not have any desire to destroy Ellie or Tommy. They were, after all, two more innocents in all of this. Yet, it was the perfect opportunity to throw a grenade into the perfect lives of those heinous hypocrites.

A few minutes later, he pulled up at the far end

of a dirt road and watched Richie enter the Gibbs riding stables. It was just one more place for him to ache as he and Lara had snuck up her many times. They hadn't just come to see the horses though there was something gentle about those masterful beasts. His footsteps fell softly as he stepped out of the car and decided to make his way round to the back of the stables and peer in. His eyes scanned for life but the only person who now appeared to be here was Richie himself. The familiar scent of hay tangled with the earthy aroma of the horses, reminding him of those years gone by. It reminded him of Lara, though there was nothing unpleasant about her aroma. Inside, Richie disappeared into the sanctuary of this equine beauty, leaving Chris on the periphery once more.

Positioned at a safe distance, Chris observed the stable entrance, anticipation coursing through his veins. He yearned for vengeance, yet the addition of Ellie into the equation had thrown him into disarray. He had no desire to hurt the one person who had loved Lara as much as he did.

In the stillness of time, Chris wondered if he had

become blinded by revenge. So blind in fact that he could not dull the feeling of rage when he saw Ellie leaning into that window. Could she know what this village had done to him and his mother's relationship, or that they drove him out of town before driving his mother to her sad empty death?

Richie emerged quite suddenly, startling Chris, and causing him to stumble away from the stables. He thought once more about his hatred. He had sought that glimmer of hope that might just poke a hole in such volatility, but it never landed. He feared that he might get to an understanding within himself one day but maybe it would be a day too late. Chris wanted revenge but he didn't want it to remain on his soul for all the rest of life. He wanted to rid himself of this darkness but now he suspected that it would never stop haunting his existence.

CHAPTER EIGHT

Ellie Hunter hadn't been able to decide whether it was better to be lonely or abused. In fact, the enigma lay like a sharp thorn digging through her flesh. She sat alone in her dimly lit living room, her strained marriage still suffocating her despite the fact she had locked Tommy out weeks ago. Still, she'd spent more than half her life tormented by him. It was difficult to adjust without searching the dark shadows for his presence.

Her phone rang, the shrill sound jolting her from her thoughts. Reluctantly, she reached for it, checking the number. She hesitated for a moment, contemplating whether to answer or ignore the call. But deep down, she knew that Tommy's persistence would only escalate if she refused to engage. It was better to get it over with, she thought.

Taking a deep breath, Ellie pressed the answer button and brought the phone to her ear, bracing herself for the well-worn manipulations. He would start off apologizing, before promising her the earth before moving onto more persuasive measures to break her spirit.

'Hello, Tommy,' she said, her voice betraying a mix of weariness and defiance.

Tommy's voice dripped with venom as he unleashed his tirade. 'You think you can keep me out of your life, Ellie? Just change the locks and that's me gone. You seem to be forgetting something.'

Ellie listened in shock because normally there was a bridge between faux kindness and his vitriol. That didn't seem to be in existence today. Her grip on the phone tightened, her nails digging into her palm. She knew she had made the right decision to separate from him, but the fear of his vindictiveness always broke her in the end.

'What do you want, Tommy?' Ellie asked, her voice trembling with a mixture of anger and fear.

A sinister chuckle echoed through the phone. 'I want my wife and kids back. You're not keeping me out of my house.'

'My house,' she snarled, a rare resolve in her voice. 'I bought it with the money my aunt Edith left to me. You're lucky if you've contributed a lick of paint in the last five years.'

He growled. 'Don't push me, Ellie.'

She recoiled, knew she'd gone too far, and she didn't want to bait him any further. It wasn't as if a door between them would keep her safe. At his worst, Tommy was fully capable of tearing the door of the hinges without breaking a sweat. The police wouldn't be able to help her because she'd learned long ago there was always someone in Tommy's corner.

'You won't get away from me. Not while you're alive.' His words hung in the air, his threat lingering like a dark cloud. Ellie's mind raced, she wasn't having him back, but she didn't know if she could stay here and keep him out.

'Tommy, why won't you let me be? You're not happy either. Why don't you find someone you'll be happy with. It's evidently not me,' she said, softly. Her voice quivered and she knew it was something she'd said many times before. It fell on deaf ears. Tommy certainly did enjoy relationships with other women, sometimes quite openly but it wouldn't force him to loosen his grip on Ellie.

Tommy's voice turned colder; his tone laced with malice. 'And who will you turn to, Ellie? One of the Gibbs boys. Or maybe you'll just head straight to the golden goose, Richie. Will you still be Connie's blue-eyed girl if she knows exactly what you've done?'

Her heart sank, the mention of Connie striking a nerve. Connie had been her rock, her closest friend in the absence of her true closest friend, and confidante. The thought of losing her support, of being exposed sent a wave of panic through Ellie's veins.

'I haven't done anything,' her voice cracking with desperation.

'Meet me down on the pier in ten minutes. If you don't show up, I will make that call. I'll tell her everything and my guess, knowing Connie is she'll tear you apart limb by limb.' His voice oozed with satisfaction and then the line went silent.

Meeting Tommy would be the worst thing she could do but she had no choice. She couldn't let him infect her life anymore. Connie was the one person who had never judged her, probably only because she had no idea who Ellie really was or what she would do to protect herself. Ellie didn't even know who she really was.

She wouldn't cry. Not now. He had weakened her enough. She had to steel herself for difficult decisions because if she stayed in this village, she feared he would always hold all the power.

Ellie rose. She knew exactly why he'd chosen the lake. Tommy liked theatrics. He knew how much she hated going down to the pier. Her best friend had drowned there, and Ellie had never fully gotten over it. Tommy had chosen there because he probably suspected that vice-like grip, he'd held for the longest time might be loosening just a little. His act was becoming more vindictive and getting her down there to destroy her with nasty words, or worse was just another of his cruel actions.

Ellie had found her voice. It was a mere whimper, but it was there and, like any muscle in the body, all she had to do was exercise it. She hoped it would become strong and eventually a force that he wouldn't reckon with. She also hoped that he didn't plan to harm her because she now suspected Tommy was capable of anything and, for some unknown reason, nobody had ever made anything stick.

*

The memories of the tragic day when Chris found Lara lifeless on the pier had never left him. He approached the familiar shoreline and compared this place to the part of North London where he lived now. That was a hub of change. There was barely a week gone by when a new building didn't go up, or a new ship opened. Crianlarich had never changed.

He saw a few figures continue their walk and recalled that way back in the day, this was the popular tourist route for the West Highland Way. Once upon his time his mother, Cathy, had taken in overnight stays to earn a little extra cash. It was a far cry from the big hotel at the crossroads of the village. He was glad to see the tradition wasn't dead.

He held a small bunch of supermarket flowers in his hand and walked towards the shoreline. It was a haunting place, but it was the last place he had held his girl, also the place he held the most memories as they used to take the speedboat out to the caverns and dive in. However, before he could reach the pier, the sound of angry voices drew his attention.

Chris got behind a climb of shrubs. He spotted Ellie standing on the pier, her figure flushed by the late afternoon sunlight. He paused, listening intently as Ellie's husband, Tommy Hunter, unleashed a torrent of furious words at her.

Their argument echoed across the stillness of the water, revealing the strained state of their marriage. Chris watched in silence as they discussed the locked doors and Tommy's forceful desire to return. Ellie's voice dripped with bitterness as she begged him not to force the issue.

As their conversation continued, Ellie mentioned the upcoming twentieth anniversary of Lara's death, a painful milestone that lay like a hatchet in the gut of all their lives. It was then things took an even nastier turn.

Hiding in the nearby shelter, Chris watched, his gaze locked on the unfolding scene. His eyes widened as he witnessed Tommy's rage manifest physically, his fist connecting with Ellie's face. He watched through tall blades as Ellie fell to the ground and let out a scream. He wanted to intervene, but he hesitated, torn between rushing to Ellie's aid and maintaining his cover in the shadows. Chris had lost too much to let someone else get in his way.

He recalled how he and Tommy had cruised this town, two best friends at odds with each other, vying for the attention of the best-looking girl. Of course, Ellie had been every bit as good-looking as Lara, but she lacked her spark, her confidence. It was sport to them, but this wasn't sport. This was abuse and it sickened Chris to know that this might have been the fate that lay out for Lara if they'd made different choices.

With gritted teeth, Chris chose restraint, biding his time in the darkness. He continued to watch as Tommy's aggression subsided, and Ellie cradled her injured face. The shadows concealed Chris's seething anger, but also forged in him a new determination. Tommy wasn't getting away with that. Even in his belief that Ellie was cheating on her husband, what he witnessed there on the pier made him furious.

Tommy stormed away, leaving Ellie to sob alone. Chris emerged from his hiding place. His steps were solid, firm, commanding even. He had witnessed the extent of Tommy's violence. Or, had he? It was another string to the bow of revenge he had plotted but was determined before the week was out, he would be confronting his former best friend and demanding answers. His visit to Crianlarich had started out simple but each passing minute and discovery further lunged him back into the hearth of life here. Something he was at odds with himself to indulge. He couldn't wait to get away from here and return to the life he had made for himself in London.

CHAPTER NINE

Dusk was due. The perfect time to follow someone and not be detected. Of course, he had fallen on Chris by accident. How the hell the man had the nerve to come back here after all these years was incomprehensible.

The young man looked into his mirror and continued to tap gently on the accelerator. He drove in third gear, determined to stay far enough back that he wouldn't risk discovery.

Where was Chris going now?

The man knew the drive. He'd taken it many times himself. He followed Chris's car along the straight narrow road towards the roundabout that split the village from the bigger nearby towns. Then, he took the first turn and followed him up the deep wind that served as the ridge of the village crest.

He passed each house, noting that he knew every person who lived in this place. Each garden was grander than the last and he took credit for that. His landscaping was the envy of anyone in a nearby town, but he had swore to keep his work contained to this village and it had never failed him or left him penniless yet.

He would have a word with Mr. Lazenby on his next visit because a mound of compost had lay in the corner of an otherwise exquisite display and, whilst not entirely dangerous, was really quite ugly.

Mrs. Brown's grass needed some colour. He would deal with that later because right now he had something darker on his mind. He wanted to know why Chris was here, taunting a family who he had already destroyed once.

He pulled up outside the large house at the top of the winding road and watched Chris get out of the car. The door slammed without caution and evidently Chris had done enough homework to know that no-one would be home. After all, even he wasn't stupid enough to forget that if fell prey to Connie's wrath, he'd be taking his life in his hands.

Watching, anger coursing like snake venom, the man waited in horror as Chris tackled the doors and then the windows at the front of the house. Then, he disappeared round the side and didn't return. A few minutes later, he appeared in the window of the dining room. He had managed to find his way in and now he was pouring through the lives of Connie and Richie.

The young man got out of the car and grabbed a wrench from the boot. He wouldn't stand by and allow Chris to hurt Connie and Richie again. He'd kill before he would allow that to happen.

*

Chris moved silently through the Gibbs house, his footsteps careful and deliberate. His search for answers had led him to this pivotal moment, where he stood amidst the remnants of a life once shared. In the absence of any real controversary or dirt online, he now combed through their belongings, seeking something to expose and destroy them with.

As he made his way to Lara's room, a rush of memories engulfed him. The door creaked open, revealing a space frozen in time. Nothing had changed since the last time he had been here, a sanctuary where they would hide from the world, a museum that kept in place their innocence before death and hatred had engulfed those closest to Lara.

As his eyes fell upon Lara's photo board, his heart sank. All the photos of him had been meticulously removed, leaving behind an empty space that mirrored the void left by Lara's absence. Anger surged within him, the realisation that he had been whitewashed from her life amplifying his sense of betrayal.

He struggled to comprehend how the memories they had shared, the love they had nurtured, could be so easily discarded. The ache of loss resurfaced, intertwined with a burning rage that demanded justice. Any doubt he had held about destroying her family was now replaced with his vow to reclaim his place in Lara's short narrative.

Of course, Chris didn't know that he wasn't alone. Someone had followed him here, they lurked in the darkness, as driven by hatred as he was. They were watching his every move.

As he reached the bottom of the stairs, his eyes darting around the room, Chris remained oblivious to the prying gaze fixed upon him. The air crackled with tension, the unknown observer silently watching and waiting.

Chris steeled himself for the battle that he knew would be here imminently. The shadows whispered promises of redemption. Unbeknownst to him, those were the very shadows that would test his mettle and push him to the brink.

CHAPTER TEN

Barbecue season was coming to an end. Connie was glad because as much as she loved having the family round, she and Drew rarely seen eye to eye. In fact, Connie much preferred the company of his wife, Stephanie. She never needed an excuse to shower love onto her two-year-old grandson though. Oliver was the little beacon of light she needed.

Besides, these gatherings never felt complete. Simon and his partner, Gordon rarely attended and of course there was the obvious absence. A gaping hole at the centre of their lives that could never be filled.

'What do you think of what they're saying about Max?'

Connie shook her head., 'What a load of rubbish. I won't believe it. Max was a good man. He helped this family out at the worst time of our lives.' She popped the cork on a bottle of red and offered it round the room. If this motley crew weren't here, she might have swigged from the bottle, but she wouldn't give her self-important son the satisfaction of casting his weary eye over her movements in judgment. So, she did the civilized thing and grabbed a glass.

'You know that they're saying he molested someone, don't you?'

She hissed. 'Molested someone. Drew, I gave you more credit than that. Yes, I've heard there's a video. Shocking. The things people can do with technology these days is incredible.'

Neither Richie nor Stephanie engaged because they were both well aware that their input was only welcome when it was what Drew or Connie wanted to hear. Two sides of the same coin split by arrogance and an unwillingness to accept the other for the person they were.

'Mum, I know you went to school with his younger sister but, for once, can you accept that someone you like might have done something wrong.'

She slammed the bottle on the counter. 'No,' she roared. 'I can/t. Can you accept that people lie about others all the time.'

He sniffed, let his shoulders sag as he threw up

his hands. 'Okay, mum. You win. He must be innocent. That's why he went up and threw himself off a bridge before anyone else had even heard the news.'

'Oh, Drew. Shut up,' she bellowed. 'Use the few brain cells I gifted you. He killed himself because some bastard decided to spread malicious lies that, if they stuck, would have destroyed his life.'

Drew stood, walked round the cradle by the backdoor and picked up his baby. 'Dad, cancel the burgers. Connie's in one of her feral moods again. She hasn't even finished the bottle yet.'

'Watch it,' warned Richie, a rare stern look that should have been enough to settle things. It wasn't.

'Dad, I know you don't want to upset her. God forbid, anyone else should have an opinion that she disagrees with. I'm not staying here to be insulted.'

'Well, go home then. Go and be insulted there.' Connie wasn't looking now. She was swigging back from the bottle, her intensely taut stance growing more rigid by the moment.

Stephanie, always able to hold her own but

beleaguered by the constant taunting, ran her hand down Connie's arm.

Connie shivered. She didn't need comforted; she needed her son to stop being a prick. She knew he had never agreed with them about what happened to Lara. He may not have swum to the dark side, but he paddled in its vicinity.

She watched Drew put Oliver's arms into his jacket just as Stephanie lifted the nappy bag. She wanted to apologise, threw out the olive branch but why should she apologise for feeling how she felt. So, she continued to sulk and turned away from Drew's scowl. They'd speak tomorrow. She didn't hold grudges, neither did he. Still, she feared that one day, he wouldn't return. Maybe he would finally tire of her trauma and decide he didn't need a mother who was evidently such a failure. When that day came, Connie hated to admit that it would be almost as bad as the day she lost her beautiful daughter.

*

Chris had always loved these stables. He loved the horses, their majestic presence proving to be balm for his worn soul. There was a sense of tranquility that washed over him, wringing out the turbulence that seemed so constant within.

With a gentle touch, he reached out to stroke the velvety muzzle of a nearby horse, feeling the warmth and trust emanating from the creature. Chris trusted animals in a way he rarely trusted people because they rarely betrayed in the same way as human beings. Though, he knew a horse of that stature would likely cause some damage to anyone who got in his way.

He remembered how Lara loved this place; her eyes twinkled every time she left the stables behind on the back legs of her great stallions. It had been a sanctuary for both of them, a world where they could simply be.

While his heart still burned with a thirst for revenge against the Gibbs family, the presence of the horses tempered his anger, reminding him of the purity that resided within these magnificent creatures. Their unwavering trust flushed him with guilt for as much as he could love them, he hadn't come here in admiration.

In the quiet of the stables, Chris reaffirmed his reasons for coming here. He clapped the large Clydesdale on his muzzle once more then he pulled back and grimaced. He walked through the stables, his feet crunching on hardened hay and unlatched each of the barn doors. Internally, Chris could not tell if he was shivering in fear, or delight. However, he pulled out the small bottle from his pocket and began to douse the bales of hay in its contents.

With a heavy sigh, he waved goodbye to the grand creatures who now trotted out into the centre of the stables. It hurt him to know he would be hurting them, but Chris needed to send a message. He needed them to know, somehow, that the message had come from him.

He got to the barn door, pulled out a packet of cigarettes from his pocket and placed one on his lower lip. He lit it and inhaled deeply before dropping the lighter flame to the ground. Then, he listened to the animal's scream as flames rushed along the side of the stables. It was a torturous sound but one that wouldn't last for long, he suspected. He turned, blew his smoke into the air, and began the short walk back to the car.

As he left the stables behind, he heard the flames crackle, but it was nothing to the scream of those poor animals as they scrambled to avoid being burnt. He got behind the wheel, already noticing the army of silhouettes in the distance. Soon it would become obvious. This was no isolated incident, and neither was the reveal that led to the death of Max McDermott. Someone was out to get them, and no living creature would be safe until the task at hand was complete.

He pressed his lips against her neck and felt the cold-water swirl round them. He had loved her since the minute they'd met. She had played a little hard to get, that teasing glint in her eye, the way she carried herself like she was twenty years old, how she spoke in little riddles that he had come to know as their own secret little language.

'How is it you get more beautiful every day?'

She threw back her head and let the moon rest on her skin. Then she said, in her own seductive way, 'How is it you get fuller of crap?'

He laughed.

The world was theirs. They were already planning their summer getaway. A flight to Athens before crossing the borders and seeing parts of Europe that had existed only in pictures for them. It was a world they hadn't known about individually but as a pair, a formidable pair, one imagination had locked into the other, like the matching of a long-lost key to a vortex untapped.

'Would you believe me if I told you I loved you?'

'No,' she said, teasing again. 'But you can say it anyway.

He reached up and grabbed the bottle of champaign from the side of the wooden boat and took a swig. Then, he passed it to her and watched as she kissed the rim with her heart-shaped lips.

'Go on, then, Christopher Lee Burns. Tell me how you love me and that you can't wait to get me to the alps so you can make love to me on the peaks.'

Chris smirked and pulled her to him. He cocked his head just enough that she could pour the fizzing contents of the bottle onto the lower half of his face. He bit forward to catch a drink. 'I don't need to take you there to do that, gorgeous. I can love you right here.'

Lara threw the bottle back into the old half-painted wreckage and pressed her hands to the back of his neck. Then, she allowed him to kiss her in a way she'd never been kissed. It was like fire and ice all at once, the sensation spreading across her face. If only this kiss could last forever.

CHAPTER ELEVEN

Ellie

Ellie awoke in a state of panic, her heart pounding against her chest as she frantically searched her surroundings. The last thing she remembered was calling her daughter, Elizabeth. She wanted to speak to Cole because it had been three days since she'd seen him, and she was becoming agitated.

Confusion swirled within Ellie's mind as she tried to remember when she'd gone to bed. She was still frightened because she couldn't think of another set-to with Tommy. Not today. Her hand gingerly touched her burst lip, a cruel reminder of his latest violent outburst. It was just the catalyst she needed to spur her forward in her escape. She couldn't tolerate his abuse any longer. He'd held her captive long enough.

As Ellie glanced around the room, her eyes landed on a small bag tucked away in the corner. It had been her hidden secret, a reserve for the road.

Soon, it would become her lifeline. She carefully packed the last of her essential belongings, silently vowing to leave behind all that had defined her.

Ellie's heart raced with both fear and hope as she stood at the threshold of her new life. The bag in her hand felt heavy with the weight of her past, but she knew it also carried the promise of a brighter future. She thought of her children, Cole and Elizabeth, and the strength they had unknowingly given her during darker moments. They were her anchor, her reason to keep going. This place had been her prison and she was at the finishing line of her sentence. She would break free from Tommy and step into the unknown, armed with the courage to rebuild her shattered life.

The difficult decisions had already been made. Elizabeth had sourced a small flat in the centre of Glasgow for Ellie and Cole. It wouldn't be sensible to join Elizabeth in Edinburgh. Not when it was likely the first place Tommy would look for them. Better to be a little off the radar, throw him off the scent so to speak.

Her bruised reflection stared back at her, but she

also noticed that she had a slice of dried blood down her arm. She hadn't noticed that when he pushed her to the ground. Ellie took a deep breath, allowing her newfound determination to permeate all the way through her.

Ellie thought of her old life. Her parents died when she was young, and she was raised by her aunt Edith. Edith was a force. She was a music teacher, a traditional eccentric who had never had her own children. It was like fate because Edith adored her only niece and Ellie barely knew her own mother. Sadly, Edith was gone now too. Her entire world had been reduced to a dependency on a brute who encaged her. She knew she had to escape because she suspected that if Tommy didn't kill her first, she would probably kill herself. If it wasn't for her children, Ellie feared she would have ended it all years ago.

She looked into the dawning sun and tried to find a fragment of hope. Maybe once she was gone from here, she could finally put her husband behind her and find some normalcy. She just didn't know how to exist without Tommy and that filled her with fear more than death itself.

CHAPTER TWELVE

Father William Brady looked out the window as he listened intently to Richie Gibbs. Not another bloody drunk sleeping it off in his grounds, he thought, continuing to hear what Richie was saying. Father Brady would rather the locals slept off the booze-fed nights inside the chapel than outside. He had other things to think about right now, though.

'Are you sure it was deliberate, Richie?'

An impertinent snort followed. 'Bill, the place stinks to high heaven of petrol.'

'Any casualties?'

'Only my business,' said Richie, flatly. 'Thankfully someone unbolted the doors, and the horses and ponies were able to escape. They were found wandering the fields, distressed, and howling. I just wonder who set them free.'

'Whoever called the fire in, I dare say,' said Father Brady, returning to the window and wondering when his latest guest was going to climb off that monument and get home.

'Who knows? Anyway, Bill, can you take a couple of them in the old stable behind the chapel? I've got a few of them homed already but I'll be all morning trying to find places for the rest of them.'

'Of course,' said Father Brady, absently. He ended the call and decided he would go and wake his unwanted visitor. He had long been past hospitable, but he would check the visitor didn't want a mug of tea.

The grass was wet and soggy, rather suggesting there had been a torrent in the night. His black shoes squelched on the sodden blades as he stomped towards the middle aisle of the small cemetery. Halfway along, though, he suddenly stopped.

Not much shocked Father William Brady. Despite his collar, he had been a man of the world. The sight of the still body, webbed in a massive spray of blood caused him to stop rigid. He moved forward and leaned over the body. Gasping, Father Brady turned away as if he might vomit in a moment.

One more glance and he knew exactly who lay dead in his cemetery. Tommy Hunter had finally met his maker and even Father Brady wasn't altogether surprised about that.

*

Ellie didn't need to wait for the knock at the door to know her husband was dead. It took all of two minutes for the police to get to the crime scene and the news spread like fanned flames in the wind.

Panic gripped Ellie's heart as the news of her husband's murder reached her ears. The world around her seemed to blur as she ran through the streets, desperate to reach the cemetery where Tommy's lifeless body had been callously discarded. Every step was fueled by a mix of fear, confusion, and a strange concoction of relief mingled with guilt.

Arriving at the grounds of the cemetery, Ellie's breath came in ragged gasps as she scanned the area. She couldn't see her husband, unsurprisingly but suspected that his dead body lay beneath the ghoulish white fabric of an erected tent.

By the time the panic subsided, a fractured clarity broke through, and she found herself imagining that any moment now she'd wake up to the sound of him trying to get through the door. A momentary response of fear, or a memory? She didn't know but she inspected the faces of those now beginning to stare and whisper.

She saw Maggie Bradley cast an eye over her before leaning in and speaking to a slim man in a grey suit. The investigating detective, no doubt.

Ellie froze because she suddenly realised after it was too late that the grey suited man was moving toward her. Could she run? What a strange reaction, she feared. What would the man possibly think?

It didn't matter anyway because he was already upon her before her feet, frozen in place had made any attempt to move. She could feel a tingle spread across her gaunt face, another panic attack perhaps. Her tongue felt thicker. Her eyes darted upwards and caught sight of moving clouds. It wouldn't have surprised Ellie if the sky came crashing down. Instead, she suspected it would be the ground that came up to meet her.

'Ellie Hunter?'

Strange that he knew her name, but she didn't

know his. 'Yes,' she muttered, desperate to grab onto the black iron fence surrounding the cemetery.

'Can I take you somewhere? Into the chapel perhaps.' His voice was perfectly even, crisp as the breeze itself. His face remained expressionless, like he'd donned a rubber mask for these occasions and would later tear it off to reveal a real human face under there.

Ellie nodded. Her mind tumbled with words, but they wouldn't string together, nor pass her lips.

'Come on, Mrs. Hunter,' he said, placing his hand gently under her elbow and forming a smile. Yet, the sudden formality was startling. 'I'm Detective Starling and I'll be leading the investigation. Firstly, let's get you warmed up. Father Brady is inside and will make you a little more comfortable.'

She turned back and tried to decipher the many familiar faces. Friends, neighbours but mostly enemies Tommy had made over the years with his bullish and illegal activity.

The world spun on its axis a little and Ellie

pressed her hand against her upper chest.

'Come on,' said the detective, loosening his tie just a smidgen enough to reveal a line of sweat had settled and curled down the lapel of his shirt.

She tightened her eyes, thwarted her tears because even in her hatred of his behaviour, she had always loved Tommy since childhood. Theirs was a co-dependency that defied her fear of him and his toxic control of her. She wouldn't let her neighbours see her cry. Nor would she break down in front of Tommy's enemies.

What really occurred to her in that moment as she held her back to the gathering crowd was that one of those enemies, someone who had crossed swords with Tommy, would most likely be responsible for murdering him. What terrified her more though was that the culprit would wonder about her and her children. Ellie knew little about her husband's dealings, but she didn't know if his killer knew that. If she didn't already have enough reasons for fleeing this snake-pit, she'd just found one more reason to run.

CHAPTER THIRTEEN

He hadn't expected it to happen so quickly. Chris watched with giddiness as Darren Phillip was forcibly escorted from his four-bedroom house near Callander. The files had been damning but even Chris couldn't have known the extent of Darren's corruption.

Chris had endured a sleepless night. He wanted his revenge, no doubt, but he also wanted to enjoy the aftermath. There had been no aftermath for Max McDermott who had taken the easy step off a bridge, imparting pain only to his poor undeserving wife and the traumatised driver of a twelve-wheeler.

Of course, Chris wouldn't allow himself to delve too deep into that because he had always considered himself a man of integrity and decency who had been forced into a grid of corruption and wrongdoing by people who portrayed themselves upstanding and kind.

He'd hit the send button on Darren's file moments after sending the video of Max into the digital stratosphere. There was a difference though because the extent of Darren's dealings would mean a lengthy prison service at best and anyway, his treatment of Chris all those years ago didn't feel so personal. No less destructive, but not personal.

MIT must have hit the motherload because they'd taken less than twenty-four hours to put together a squad. Perhaps Chris's material had been just the icing on an already baked cake. The material was wealthy though; blackmail, murder, corruption, cyber-fraud, and that was only what Chris had put together in a few short months. The sharp tip of a very long iceberg.

There was a surge of exhilaration as his lips curled into a triumphant smile. Chris felt satisfied because he knew Darren wouldn't have an out. There was no towering bridge of speeding traffic where he was going. He was going to face what he had done to Chris and to all those others he had destroyed over the years.

Later, Chris would learn of the extent of Darren's criminal activities and illegal ventures. The dead bodies were plentiful, the skeletons all waiting to fall out of an endless closet. A surge of pride rushed through Chris though as he watched Darren protest, then an officer pushing his head down until he was forced into the back seat of a marked car.

Nobody would thank Chris. He would just be a ghost in cyberspace. However, he wanted just a moment of glory. It might have been careless, but he didn't care. After all, he'd only just gathered the data. He hadn't been responsible for the crimes. So, he stepped out of the car and walked to the house next door. He perused the cul-de-sac and noted the other faces watching with grave interest. None of them would know who he was. In fact, he suspected the only person who would recognise him was Darren himself.

Two figures emerged from the house with boxes of material. They were moving towards a van where the evidence of Darren's thirty-year illegal prominence would most likely be scoured over with meticulous precision. Right now, though, Chris moved as far as he was allowed to go and placed himself directly in Darren's eyeline.

There wasn't immediate recognition. After all, Chris was still hiding behind this beard and Darren hadn't aged well. He was probably only a few years older than Chris, but he could have been sixty.

Chris smiled, his grin widening.

Moving forward in the back seat of the police car, Darren lifted his handcuffed hands and pressed them against the window. His eyes blazed, recognition finally setting in. He drew back his lips as the lower one began to tremble in anger.

Darren might have wondered what had driven Max McDermott to his death yesterday but right now, Chris suspected he was more interested in what had been done to him.

Lifting his hand to wave gently, Chris nodded his head victoriously. He could still taste the humiliation of waking up all those years ago inside the boot of Darren's car and being dragged into the woods. He could still hear the gunshot that was fired off in warning as they'd ordered him to get out of this village. Chris has been branded a killer, even though he'd never harmed a hair on Lara's head. Now, he knew that the only killer here was Darren and it pleased him to know that the bastard would finally answer for all the evil he'd done.

*

Ellie's mind whirled with a myriad of thoughts and emotions. She found the chapel house a peaceful place and was glad of Father Brady's gentle repose. It was easier to contemplate the countless possibilities that could have ended Tommy's life so abruptly.

Something else clawed at her thoughts though. Amidst the chaos of her thoughts, a sudden image of Chris materialized in her mind. The very notion that he might have killed on her behalf sent a shiver down her body. It was a notion she pondered quietly as her eyes fixed on a flickering candle which cast dancing shadows on the Chapel walls. However, she couldn't shake off that nagging suspicion that Chris might have stepped in to protect her. She hadn't asked for it, but could she really be ungrateful?

'Are you okay? Can I do anything for you?'

Ellie had forgotten Father Brady was even in the room. She felt his hand placed on her shoulder and she simply shook her head. Speech was difficult now because she didn't know if she would say the wrong thing. She had to speak to Chris. Where would she find him though?

'You know, Ellie. Sometimes people do bad things. I hear them all the time in the confessional. The reasons are always very different, but the guilt is often the same. If you ever feel that you wanted to talk to me in that capacity, please know that I am bound by God to keep it secret.'

Ellie wasn't sure how true that was. She wasn't a religious woman. After all, God had failed her more times than she could count so she didn't hold much faith in him, but she did appreciate the wise counsel from Father Brady. She wondered if he held the same suspicions about her as she did about Chris.

'Thank you, Father. God and I have never been on great terms, but I appreciate your kindness. I think I have to just go home and call my children. I hope nobody has contacted them before I can break the news.'

'Are you sure it's not something you would like

my support in?'

Gathering her courage, Ellie stood up and smiled. Her nerves continued to jangle. 'This is something I'd prefer to do alone. Just between the three of us.' She made her way out of the chapel house, her steps determined yet filled with trepidation. Her to-do list seemed to expand by the second. She had to call Elizabeth and Cole, she had to get to Chris and find out if he had something to do with this, work needed to be called and, lastly, she had to call Tommy's mother in Spain. It was a phone call she hated to even think of because she could already imagine the histrionics and she would be expected to participate. Tommy's mother was almost as awful as he was, and Ellie wasn't entirely confident she could be gentle.

Ellie walked past Chris's house and saw it was in the same darkness it had remained in since Cathy's death. She stopped perfectly still and wondered if he was even living here at the moment. Maybe he'd opted to be somewhere else. She spun round, grabbing the gate and staring across the street. Her heart sank as she noticed the figure in a nearby doorway.

Suddenly, the list of potential killers expanded. Maybe Chris wasn't the only one who could have taken action to protect Ellie. Or perhaps the person who had snuffed Tommy's life out had an altogether different agenda.

She drew breath, tightened up her shoulders and began the short walk to the other side of the street.

CHAPTER FOURTEEN

Ryan and Maggie stood at the edge of the cemetery, the lingering sunlight casting long shadows over the tombstones. The crime scene continued to grow, each new figure checking in with a young officer with a clipboard.

Dr. Wilson, the chief forensic pathologist, joined them near the tent, a somber expression on his face. The grass all around the area had become sodden beneath the constant footfall, further evidence of the intense investigation that had taken place.

Introductions happened with Dr. Wilson eying the young DI wearing an expression of mild suspicion. 'Maggie, nice to see you,' he said, coyly. 'The family all well?'

'Gerry is fine, still as cantankerous as ever. The boys are in their twenties, both at university and seeing nice girls. They still think there's a money tree in the garden and that it regenerates itself when they bleed it dry.'

'Sounds wonderful,' he said, smiling but fixing

his gaze on Ryan.

'Yes, well, what can you tell me?'

Dr. Wilson's smile faded. It seemed he already had the measure of Ryan.

Of course, the mistrust appeared to be mutual. Ryan moved to the entrance of the tent, satisfied he'd already dealt with the presence of Ellie but not realizing she had made a sharp exit almost immediately after he deposited her with the priest.

'It's very simple really. He wasn't killed here. His body was moved post-death. There is no splattering of blood beyond his clothing. The blood also appears to have come from a single stab wound in the right of his upper abdomen.'

'One stab wound?' Ryan looked in and saw that the bloody shirt appeared to be shredded. 'Are you sure?'

'Yes. I am sure that the cause of death was a deep stab wound. It was a single, fatal blow. There were more stab wounds delivered after death, but they would have been futile and unlikely to draw blood.'

Maggie, who had remained impassive until now,

shuddered. The colour drained from her face and she turned away before they forced her to stare at the body too long. She stepped to the side, forcing a split between her eyes and the macabre view inside the tent.

'Are you alright, Maggie?'

Ryan ignored the question. He didn't understand the aversion to blood. Every species on earth had it in their body. Those in a profession like theirs should have been at ease with it but it seemed many people made a dramatic display of their distaste. 'Any signs of defensive wounds or a struggle?'

'We won't know more until we do a proper examination, but I would say the fatal wound inflicted was probably a defensive wound. Perhaps it was the victim who attacked his killer, and they were defending themselves.'

Maggie sighed knowingly.

Ryan less inclined to draw conclusions this early. He didn't personally know Tommy Hunter, didn't know his background and hadn't yet been introduced to the plethora of criminal activities he'd been questioned over. Not that it mattered. The police weren't in power to make judgements. They gathered evidence and handed it over so someone else could make the final decision.

'I will say it was swift though. He must have been dead within seconds because the subsequent wounds would likely have happened within minutes but none of them show any indication of blood matter or that they impacted on life extinction.'

'How many?'

'How many what?'

Ryan saw the surprise in both Dr. Wilson and Maggie's faces. Was he too brutal? Not enough emotion, perhaps. 'Stab wounds. We know the first blow proved fatal which begs the question why anyone should inflict any more. It screams of brutality, an emotional response perhaps. How many times was he stabbed after he was already dead?'

'Seventeen in total, including the first fatal wound.'

Ryan's thoughts drifted to the harrowing scene before them, and he wondered why someone would choose this place in particular. A place of stillness had suddenly become a theatre of death, a showcase of bloody violence.

'What about DNA evidence?'

Dr. Wilson laughed, a hearty response that cut through the tension of the situation. 'You watch too many shows on television, Maggie. Murders aren't usually resolved that quickly and we don't get all the results in a few days.'

'I know that,' she said, flushing slightly because she felt silly.

Ryan was annoyed. He didn't know Maggie very well, but he liked what he knew about her. In the few short months since he'd arrived here, she had mothered him. He'd even met her husband, Gerry, when she insisted he come over for Sunday dinner. Ryan didn't like Sunday dinner and he especially didn't like company, but the Bradley's were nice hosts, and he appreciated the effort. 'It must be nice to know everything,' he said, sharply and turned away.

Maggie followed him. 'You didn't have to be

rude. I've known Nigel a long time. He was only joking.'

Ryan didn't care. Nor did he care that Maggie was annoyed at him. 'He was rude. Talking down to you in that lofty tone. You didn't deserve that. I understand you don't get many murders round these parts. He should be teaching, not gloating.' He stopped and looked back. 'I just hope his work is as quick as his wit.'

Maggie rolled her eyes. 'You're not exactly au fait with social etiquette yourself, young man. It would do you well to be a little more polite, even when you don't appreciate someone's comments. Nigel and I have been thrown together for work for thirty years and he's one of Gerry's golfing friends.'

Ryan knew it was not an argument he would win. He had upset Maggie by defending her. He would never understand people and their loyalties. Then again, he suspected that Tommy had been murdered in a deep-seated rage and that they would probably learn it had been perpetrated by someone he had been loyal to.

'By the way,' continued Maggie, her expression softening. 'Did you see the name on the grave that Tommy's body was left on?'

Ryan suspected he wouldn't be at all familiar with the name on the tombstone, but he was momentarily amused by Maggie's flare for the dramatic. 'Who?'

'You know Connie and Richie Gibbs?'

'Yes,' he continued.

'Well, their daughter died in a tragic drowning accident many years ago. The grave that Tommy was dumped on belongs to Lara Gibbs.'

*

Ellie's heart skipped a short beat, then another and another. The palpitations were common now. She knew when panic was about to take over and she often found that she could control it if she caught it just at the right time.

She was crossing the road, dazed by the events over the past few days and guilty that when she did eventually deliver the news of Tommy's death to her lovely children, she would be secretly hailing her new life.

There was no bond bar the one with her children that Ellie held sacred more than the one with Connie Gibbs. As she approached the shop front, she felt the weight of unspoken words and she found herself wondering; Was it possible she had gotten it so wrong? Could Connie be the killer? As she drew closer, she noticed the remnants of tears glistening on Connie's cheeks, a silent testament to the pain she had endured.

'Oh god, Connie. What's happened? Are you okay?'

There was no mistaking the depth of sorrow in Connie's expression because they echoed the depth of pain etched into Ellie's own wounded soul.

'The stables... they were burnt down last night,' Connie murmured, her voice strained with sadness. 'Thank god no one was hurt and that our horses managed to escape.'

Ellie felt shock ripple through her body and for a moment she forgot that this woman might have been responsible for murdering her husband. She stepped inside the shop and for one brief moment she was comforting Connie, instead of accepting comfort from her.

'Why were you going there?'

Ellie turned, caught short for an answer. 'Where?' Did she look guilty?

'To Cathy Burns' house. No-one lives there.'

Ellie stuttered. She was trying to search for the words because the words she did not dare say to Connie at this present moment was that Chris was back and that she had already spoken with him. Nor did she want to say that Chris was just one person she suspected of killing Tommy. One of many.

'Are you okay, sweetheart?'

Ellie got behind the counter, just as she had done many times since the shop opened. 'I don't know how I should feel,' she admitted.

'Nobody can blame you if you feel relieved,' said Connie, reaching forward and stroking her face. 'You deserve happiness, and I don't think Tommy was ever capable of giving you that.' Her face hardened as she pulled Ellie into a tight embrace.

Guilt! Purging her of any other emotion because there were so many things happening that felt outwith her control.

'Have the police questioned you yet?'

Ellie hadn't spoken to the detective since the moment he'd abandoned her to Father Brady. She worried that if she spoke to him too early she might unravel and that couldn't happen. Ellie wanted her escape. She wanted out of here. Even with Tommy dead she would never feel free if she remained in Crianlarich. There were too many reminders that her life had been in tatters since the death of her best friend.

Connie continued to run her hand across Ellie's poker straight hair. She always did have a calming presence, even in the wake of her own daughter's death but Ellie knew that beneath that exterior lay a tumult of rage that might pour out onto everyone else any day. Especially with the twentieth anniversary looming closer.

'You never did say why you were going to the Burns' house.'

Ellie thought the subject was closed. She hadn't found an answer that either of them would be convinced by. In the end, she settled for half a truth. 'Everyone's gone but me. Lara died, Chris left and now Tommy's gone. Is it bad that I miss what used to be?'

Connie pulled away, her eyes glazing over and the scent of alcohol escaping her breath for the briefest moment. 'It isn't bad that we latch onto the past. Sometimes it's all we have but you cannot because there's nothing there for you, Ellie. Lara will always be here,' she continued, pressing on Ellie's heart. 'Those other two, not worth your tears. I know you're probably in shock, but you must see, Ellie. This is your way out. Once the funeral is by with, you'll be able to get on with your life. Leave the past where it belongs.'

Ellie moved to the back room and grabbed herself some water. 'Are you able to leave the past behind?'

Connie sighed. 'No,' she whispered. 'It's different for me. I know we all lost Lara, but I carried that little dot of a person in my womb for nine months. Losing her has almost destroyed me. My boys are fully grown and live their own lives. Richie has barely left my side since Lara died but it can feel suffocating.' She walked to the window and let the sun rest on her face.

Ellie sipped from the glass and watched the beautiful woman in her middle-ages bask in the glow of the outside world that she now felt so bitterly aggrieved by.

'Everything that was wonderful in my life happened before Lara's death. Your slice of wonderful is yet to come. Get out there and find out. It'll never come to you here.'

Ellie sidled up to her, two women a generation apart whose lives had been destroyed by one inescapable tragedy. Ellie contemplated the wisdom of telling Connie about Chris but then she allowed this moment to sprawl because it felt like the last time they'd be together in this way.

'You've been like a mother to me.'

Connie nodded. 'Yes, I have, and I've never

regretted a moment of it. You were young when your parents died. Lara begged me to adopt you which I couldn't do because your aunt was still alive and loved you so much.'

'Would you have adopted me?'

There wasn't a moment of pause or even the slightest hint that she might have rejected Ellie. 'In a heartbeat, sweetheart. In the end I didn't have to because you've become part of the family anyway. Not every bond comes from blood, you know.'

Ellie thought of Tommy, now cold up in the cemetery and she wondered if she wasn't just a little too cold. It wasn't in her to wish someone dead, but could she really be so sad about the death of a man who would have cut off her air if she'd waited long enough.

'I love you, Ellie. I hope wherever you go now, you'll know that. You and the kids mean the world to all of us.'

Finally, the dam broke. Ellie pressed her hand to her mouth and began to wail. 'What have I done?'

Connie hushed her. Pressed her finger to Ellie's

mouth. 'Whatever you've done, it stays between us. Admit nothing. Do you understand?'

Ellie didn't know what she would confess to anyway. She had no recollection of the previous night. However, she had spent the entire morning with the vaguest fear that perhaps she hadn't been looking in the right place. It was easy to suspect those who wanted to protect her the most. Maybe the person who had protected her in the end was herself. It seemed unlikely but the more the minutes passed, the more she believed that it was a very real possibility. She looked at Connie in horror, tears still flowing and allowed the silent knowing to form a shroud around them.

CHAPTER FIFTEEN

There were few things as exhilarating for the constabulary as a rare murder in a rural area. That's how Ryan perceived it, at least. Having spent most of his career in Edinburgh, he found death to be a monotonous affair. But in the short time he had been in this small village, he had observed that most of the officers were perpetually bored and disheartened by a job that rarely extended beyond gnome-napping incidents and vandalism of public flowerbeds. Despite finding it slightly disturbing, Ryan took pleasure in witnessing the officers' newfound zeal and the atmosphere of determination and urgency that permeated the investigation room, as they voraciously absorbed every detail.

'I need someone out in the community. We need to reassure the people in this village. The last thing we need is hysteria,' Ryan said.

Maggie, on her sixth cup of coffee for the day, let out a loud slurp before laughing. 'Hysteria? You'll get a bigger reaction from the sheep. It's not George

Square or Piccadilly Circus. Most people here already know about Tommy's death. They won't be expecting it to happen to anyone else.'

'Well, that's okay then. Mystery over. Shall I hand my badge to Agnes in the cleaning department, and she can conduct my investigation?'

'There's no need to be so bloody sarcastic,' she fumed.

He turned to the room. 'I will tell you all the same thing. Do not discuss the details of this case outside this room. This is an evidence room, not a newsroom. We collect evidence and we protect it so we can build as good a case for the procurator fiscal as possible. Any breaches will be reported. Does everyone understand this?'

A voice from the gallery called out, nervously asking the question that most of the room probably wanted to ask. 'Not even at home?'

'Especially not at home,' he roared, a rare lift from his generally even temper. 'How many cases are lost because Detective Idiot told Mrs. Idiot who told Mrs. Nosey next door. Tell no-one anything while we are investigating. I cannot believe I have to even say this to a room full of police officers.'

A collective sigh broke the tension, and the buzz returned to the room.

Ryan turned back to the board, his face taut with focus, and examined the images of the victim's body post-death. 'Seventeen stab wounds,' he muttered. 'Why seventeen?'

Maggie joined him, her curiosity evident as she followed his gaze to the board. 'Why does the number matter?'

'I'm just thinking aloud, exploring my thoughts. I don't know if it's relevant. It might have been fifteen or thirty. I don't know if it matters,' he said, a flickering tic appearing at the side of his eye. 'A killer's mind can often be warped by detail. It depends on whether Mr. Hunter has been targeted by someone with a desire for the cryptic or if it's purely circumstantial.'

Maggie gave him a look of approval. 'I never thought of it like that.'

Glancing once more at the digital images

displayed on the newly installed glass screen, showcasing the victim's face, a strand of hair, and an image of the deceased's wife, Ryan felt a familiar excitement. He had always loved this part of his job—piecing together the puzzle. However, he found the early stages of an investigation frustrating, and he particularly disliked it when someone encroached on his space and asked what he deemed to be stupid questions.

He turned to the room. He looked at Tommy's police record and began to assign tasks to his team. He understood their excitement and if he were a man with better social skills, he might have felt some guilt about berating them. However, he hated tittle-tattle, even when it was to the benefit of his work. He also hated unprofessionalism and he wouldn't stand for anyone compromising his trail of evidence.

'Did you know about his arrests for domestic abuse?'

Maggie shrugged. 'I have a vague recollection of them. Everyone knows he abused his wife. He didn't bother to conceal it. She's a lovely girl. She's already had her share of heartbreak, though I would doubt getting away from Tommy, however it might have happened, would constitute heartbreak. I shouldn't think those arrests matter. She didn't press charges and I very much doubt she could get the better of him in such a way that she could inflict those wounds.'

'Everything matters. You'd be amazed at what a person can do when they're pushed to their limits. What about this here?' He pointed further down the screen.

Maggie moved inwards and pulled a chair over. The rest of the room had already dispersed, noisily excited by their quest to bring Ryan something, anything that would get them some recognition.

'I've never seen that before. I never knew anything about it,' said Maggie.

'How can you not know?' He didn't mean it as a criticism. He was genuinely perturbed that a woman as sharp as Maggie and who oversaw at the local station would not know about something so vital.

'I've never seen it before. He certainly wasn't brought to us. Look, it was overturned,' she said, pointing to the words at the bottom of the screen.

'A drug smuggling charge at the border that doesn't result in some sort of repercussions. Something isn't right there.'

Maggie nodded in agreement. 'I've never heard anything about it. He wasn't brought here. I wouldn't have known about it if it wasn't flagged to us.'

'It smells off. The big names in that game with flashy lawyers can evade us often but somebody like Tommy with a petty arrest list walking through border control at an international airport with 10 kilos of cocaine in his backpack and getting caught, well that's just a bit fishy.' He felt the tic at his eye begin to pulse harder as it did when he felt irritable.

Maggie was staring curiously, tapping on the right hand of the screen so it continued to move downwards. 'Oh my god,' she finally said, letting out a gasp.

'What is it?'

'Look at who got him out every time.'

Ryan moved to her side so their faces were almost skin to skin.

'Max McDermott saved his bacon all three times.'

*

Chris drove Ellie away from the village, their journey basked in an uneasy silence. Part of her mind focused continuously on poor Connie, a woman who had been like her mother but who she suspected could be capable of killing someone.

Not that it mattered because Ellie didn't even know that she wasn't a killer herself. How could she trust others when she didn't trust herself. Did Tommy come to the house the night before? She recalled an argument but wasn't sure if it was by telephone or in person. Perhaps she had drank too much wine. Now she was paying a formidable price.

Then, there was Chris. Twenty years after he disappeared from their lives, his return felt as surreal as everything else that had happened today.

'What's on your mind?'

Ellie didn't have the energy to lie anymore. Her conversation with Connie had drained the last ounce of energy she had. 'Did you kill Tommy?'

Silence filled the car before he finally laughed. 'No, did you want me to?'

Ellie turned to him, saw the sun redden the curled hairs on his beard. 'What kind of question is that?'

'Normally, I would say an odd one but I'm sitting in the car with a woman who has evidently been destroyed by her abusive husband. Did you kill him?' He was turning the question back on her, evidently. Behind the facial hair, a teasing smile had formed, revealing slightly discoloured teeth.

'No,' she said, wondering if she sounded convincing. 'I don't think so.' She settled back in the passenger's seat, felt the sweating leather on the back of her neck.

'I don't think you did either,' he concluded, putting a full stop on the conversation.

Ellie lowered her window and allowed the breeze to circulate throughout the car.

Chris pulled a cigarette from a pack and opened his own window. He placed it between his lips and lit it up.

'I don't remember you smoking,' said Ellie.

He shrugged. 'Just one of my many vices, I'm afraid.' He inhaled and then leaned towards the window and let it drift outwards. 'How long has he been hitting you?'

Ellie didn't want this conversation. After all, one truth might lead to another, and she wasn't sure she was ready to go there with Chris. 'Long enough,' she simply replied. Her troubled gaze must not have been lost on him because he didn't ask her anything else. She was more interested in him, anyway.

Chris stopped the car. 'Ask me.'

'Ask you what?'

'Whatever it is that you want to ask me. A lot of things have changed but the one thing that hasn't changed is you, Ellie. If there's something on your mind, I want to hear about it.'

She was taken aback by his frankness because it didn't fit with her belief that he was here for reasons other than what he claimed. There was an undercurrent. Sure, he might be selling his family home, but he could have done that from a distance. Which made her think of all that had taken place in the village in the past few days. She paused, eyeing her surroundings and it made her question how all that had happened to her in the passing years could contaminate such surrounding beauty. 'Did you have something to do with what happened to Max McDermott?'

'Yes,' he replied. 'I knew the man was a leper twenty years ago when he destroyed my life. Now everybody else knows.'

Her voice trembled as she wondered if he had any concept of the enormity of what he'd done. It sent spasms of fear through her body because she wondered how far he planned to go. 'It's not just his life you've destroyed.'

'I know.'

'I don't think Max ruined your life. I think Lara's death ruined your life and I'm not sure you would have stuck around afterwards even if they hadn't tried to blame you. You wouldn't have existed in this tiny fishbowl with people wagging fingers or pouring pity onto you.'

'Don't I get the option though? Max came after

me. You know him and his henchmen dragged me off and threatened to shoot me.'

Her eyes widened. She hadn't known that. 'I understand your anger. I'm angry about my life and what Tommy has done to me but getting revenge and hurting people doesn't fix it.'

'Doesn't it?' He was looking at her with concentrated curiosity now.

She could feel his stare, the heated glare of a man who had grown into the face of intensity and a vicious depth within him that she could never fully comprehend. 'I didn't kill Tommy. You said you believed me.'

Chris chuckled. 'I do believe you. If you didn't kill him though, then someone else did. Maybe you planted the seed, maybe you directly asked. People like Tommy don't die for no reason.'

'Are you sad about it?'

Chris shook his head. 'I could have been but when I saw what he was doing to you. He's lowlife, scum of the earth, Ellie. Sorry to speak about him like this because I know he's your husband and whatever he might have done, you don't stay married to somebody all these years and not have feelings but what Tommy was doing, it wasn't right.'

'What you're doing isn't right, either Chris. Why can't you move on?'

'It feels right. If you look at the bigger picture, Ellie, you'll understand why I have to.'

'Who's next?'

'Already done,' he said, his face now concealed behind the smoke.

It was just cryptic enough to re-ignite her suspicions. Did he mean Tommy? He'd sworn he hadn't killed him but could Ellie trust someone who was here on this awful question for vengeance. 'Where do I fit in to all this?'

'You're the only person in this shit-hole I care a crap about,' he finally confessed.

She shuddered and felt the enormity of what he was saying. 'What about Connie and Richie? Are they in your grand scheme?'

'Yes,' he said, matter-of-factly.

'They lost their daughter,' she said, indignation

seething through her words.

'Do you think I don't know their loss. I can't compete with them losing her but who can understand losing someone you love that much more than me? And you, Ellie. You lost her too. Don't you feel aggrieved that your grief has been reduced to a mere token. Crumbs from their table.'

It was incredible. He had taken a truth and warped it so badly that he sounded convinced and might have convinced her but the two people she would never want to hurt was Connie and Richie and she wasn't sure what she could do to prevent him from targeting them.

'Don't do it, Chris. You won't feel any better. You won't get the closure you think you're going to get. I mean, how do you feel about Max killing himself?'

'Satisfied,' his eyes dipping.

She sniffed and gave a half-hearted smile. 'I don't believe you. That's not the Chris I know. The Chris I know wanted to become a doctor, to help people, to make the world better, not uglier. You've had a momentary high but when you go away and you think about all the misery you've brought to Rainie McDermott, to the Gibbs and anyone else you've targeted, I think you'll just feel empty.'

He bit down on his lip. 'That Chris is dead. This is who I am. I need to know that in the end I defended myself and defended my mother.'

She heard the bitterness in his voice and took a moment to remember poor Cathy, a frail woman at the best of times and it almost broke her heart. 'What happened to you and your mum wasn't fair. I know that. Neither is this, Chris. There's been enough. You'll never get your mum back, but you should know how proud she was that you'd gone off and done something else with your life. She was glad you didn't live in anger.'

'She told you that?'

Ellie smiled, hoping for a breakthrough. 'I visited her often. We would have tea in the garden. It was a peaceful place where Tommy had never looked. He didn't know so I was able to go there just to get away.'

'She said she was proud of me?'

Ellie looked across and was certain she saw his cheeks glisten in the sunlight, but it was a mere moment just long enough that it cast doubt. Was she looking for something that didn't exist? 'Of course. She didn't choose what happened any more than you did.'

'She could have defended me.'

Ellie laughed loudly then, almost mockingly. 'Defend you. She couldn't even defend herself. You know how feisty Connie was, and still is. You know how much support the Gibbs family have around the village and elsewhere. Your mum did what she could. She told them you would never harm Lara and begged that if you came home, they leave you be.'

He didn't speak then. He flicked the cigarette butt away and threw open the car door. It was a moment of revelation because it appeared he had believed his mother betrayed him in some way and Ellie knew she never would have.

Her thoughts went back to her own troubles. It was less than twenty-four hours since Tommy's death. How could she possibly tell another human that she wasn't devastated? In her mind, she imagined Chris telling her that the devastation would come. She was just in shock, he would say. If only that were true.

Chris broke the silence then with the same question she expected she would have to continue answering for a long time to come. 'Why didn't you leave him? Why did it go on so long?'

She turned and snickered. 'Why is it always a woman's fault that she's beaten? Like we just stand there and give permission. It may shock you to know that I was actually bloody frightened that he would kill me and one day, I think he really would have.'

He held up his hands and touched her shoulder. 'I'm sorry, I'm sorry,' he insisted. 'I didn't realise. I hope you understand I only ask because I would never lift a hand to a woman so it's foreign to me that somebody would do it.'

'Chris, you're responsible for the death of a man. I think we've moved past the point of morality.' She joined him at the front of the car. 'Why did you bring me here anyway?'

'I wanted to tell you everything. I wanted you to understand.'

'Why?'

They both rested on the bonnet.

'I didn't know how much you meant to me until I saw you. You were Lara's best friend. Every memory I have of her is interlocked with you. The nights out, the hungover days where we lay about in Lara's bedroom, the drives, the boat rides. You were there for all of it. I want to know you understand why I have to do this.'

'I don't.' She didn't share in Chris's hatred for everyone else. She was too filled with hostility already to fit anyone else in. She recalled the conversation with Connie earlier and the lies she had told. Did she even know what the truth was anymore? 'My hope for you Chris is that you find peace some other way, but I don't believe you will if you see this through.'

Chris put his arm round her shoulder and stared

up into the skyline. Then, he pulled a small tablet device from inside his jacket pocket and handed it to her. 'Code is 1357. Take a look. There are people in this village who have destroyed any chance I had to grieve for Lara. In doing that, they also ruined our friendship, Ellie. I want you to know why I've done the things I've done.'

'Max?'

He looked wistful then. He frowned as the sun settled on his skin, giving it a bronze sheen that cut through the redness of his beard and brought a sparkle to his green eyes.

Ellie had forgotten how handsome he was. After all, she had her eye on him before she'd fallen for Tommy. Before he'd become besotted with Lara. A memory sparked then. She quickly buried it because she would never allow herself to revisit it. She tapped on the screen and looked at the boxes on the desktop.

'Max wasn't the first,' she whispered.

'Nope. He wasn't. He was just the most prominent. This wasn't concocted yesterday. I've been looking at these people for years. It's only now

I've found out enough to bring them down.'

She turned to him and handed him back the device. 'I don't want to see any of this.' She suddenly felt overwhelmed, like the sky and the horizon were reducing, folding in like the edge of boxes until she began to suffocate.

In a moment of desperation, Ellie turned and ran, her heart pounding in her chest. Fear propelled her forward, her mind racing to comprehend the depths of the revenge that Chris had orchestrated. She needed time to process the implications of Chris's actions.

As her footsteps echoed in the distance, she saw that he wasn't following her. He was trusting her, she suspected. Who would she tell anyway? She was too busy trying to run from herself and the knowledge that she may have committed a murder. Once her own house of cards came tumbling down, she knew she didn't want to tie herself up in his malignancy.

CHAPTER SIXTEEN

Her bond with Lara would forever define her but Connie loved her boys dearly. Since the death of Lara when Drew was fifteen and Simon was thirteen, there had been an unwritten divide. On one side of the invisible net, Richie, and Drew, both with similar natures and looks. Then, there was Simon, ever devout and faithful to her. He also looked like his father, tall and good looking, but his skin was sallower, and his eyes dipped in a sadness that always made her ache.

Dinner out had been cancelled. Mainly because Drew had called and suggested they come to the house again. It was becoming wearisome, but the last time Connie suggested some space from her son, Richie almost combusted. He insisted he would never tell his son he wasn't welcome. Which was not at all what Connie was suggesting in the first place.

She said nothing now.

The walk to Simon's house near the front of the lake was short and stifling. She knew Simon was sensitive so she opted to protect him as often as she could. She was thankful he had found Gordon, someone not as headstrong as the Gibbs family but also able to stand his own in a discussion. She liked that. Also, Gordon was a looker. Just like her boy.

She pulled at the strap of her tiny handbag and felt the leather slide through her fingers. She eyed the hills in the distance, now quivering in the late afternoon heat. The sun continued to scorch, burning off the clouds and any hope that a thunderstorm might break the monotony of this heat.

'Mum, what are you doing here?'

Connie was surprised when she saw him smile, the corner of his dark lashes turning down as he pulled her in the door. 'Now I can't visit my boys?'

'Seeing as you come armed with cake,' he said, pointing to the apple pie now poking out of the pocket of her handbag.

She smacked his arm. 'What's made you so perky? I was expecting to come here...' She paused, remembering how it irritated her when others commented on her mood.

'Expecting me to be either in the doldrums or on the ceiling? Surprise!'

She followed him past a set of burning candles on an oak cabinet in the hallway. As she entered the kitchen, she could smell the aroma from the coffee machine. She eyed Gordon standing with his back to her as he stirred rapidly, the spoon clattering against the ceramic mug.

'Gordon. How are you, sweetheart?'

He spun quickly, evidently surprised to see her. 'I'm so sorry, I didn't hear the doorbell.'

'I didn't ring it.'

Simon piped up then. 'No, I caught her at the door before she woke the dog. The neighbours have already complained that he got under their fence. The longer he sleeps the happier I'll be.'

'Then, he'll be up all night for you,' said Gordon.

Simon shrugged. 'Then he'll be nocturnal like me.' He grabbed a mug from a glass cabinet and began to make another coffee. The machine hissed as he banged around searching for sweeteners. 'I can't remember how you take this, Mum. It's been so long since you've came over.'

'It's been so long since I've been invited,' she said, good-humouredly.

Gordon threw his hands up. 'You're family. You don't need to be invited, Connie.'

She climbed onto one of the bar stools at the island and clasped her hands. 'Call me old-fashioned. My mother brought me up to wait until I was invited and never to impose without calling ahead.'

'Yet, here you are,' snarked Simon.

'Well, anyway, I came here to invite you both over. Dad has decided he wants another barbecue. I swear I'll be glad when the winter comes.'

'He'd still fry a steak in the snow,' said Simon.

'Yes, but at least I wouldn't be forced out into it. Anyway, we were supposed to be going to the pub for our dinner, but Drew invited himself again. I am starting to think they don't have any food in their freezer.'

'Weren't they round last night?'

'Well, there's not a famine on how often you're allowed to visit your parents, Simon. Despite what you think. Anyway, it would be nice if you both came. It's been a long time since we all ate together.'

Simon slid the steaming mug in front of her and then proceeded to roast up one for himself. 'Gordon is away for a few nights. I'm going to take him down to the airport, but dad said you wanted us over for Sunday dinner. Could we leave it until then?'

Gordon made his excuses and slipped past her. He had to pack a case though Connie wasn't really listening. She was more focused on her son.

'Drew called. He said he upset you last night?'

'Did he? I don't remember.' She blew into the mug and dipped her eyelids.

'It's Lara's anniversary soon. You always get a little…,' his voice trailed off.

'You want to say a little mad, don't you?'

'No, we don't use that word, remember? I'm just saying it gets hard at this time of year and this will be a big one.'

She learned forward, her heart throbbing in her chest. 'There are no small ones, Simon. Every year is a big one, a reminder of another year without her.'

'I know, Mum. I didn't mean it like that.'

She pursed her lips and forced a smile. She tensed up, anger at Drew threatening to surface. 'So, what exactly did he say?'

Gordon returned to the doorway. 'Simon, should we leave in fifteen minutes? I don't want to risk being late and missing my flight.'

Nodding his head, Simon sidled up to his mother. 'He is worried about you. He said he could smell alcohol when you got out of the car and that you became quite upset when he asked if you were still going to the cemetery.'

'Not upset, just annoyed. Who is he to tell me when I should or shouldn't visit my daughter's grave? And no, he couldn't smell alcohol on me. He could smell alcohol rub because, unlike you filthy beggars, I clean my hands.'

Silence filled the room for the shortest moment, but it felt like forever passed before one of them broke it.

'Mum, we all know how you feel.'

She threw back her head before he could

continue, and a guttural laugh echoed through the kitchen. 'Simon, let me tell you something. I lost a sister when she was in her twenties, so I know how devastating that is. Let me also assure you that it doesn't compare a fraction to what it feels like for your child to die. So, I know what this is like for you but please don't insult me by telling me that Lara's death is the same for all of us. I lost the first person I carried in my womb. If I lived a thousand years, I'd never find the words to describe how it feels.' She bit back the urge to scream, or cry. Whichever came first.

'I'm sorry,' he said, meekly.

Connie grabbed his hand tight. 'Sweetheart, you don't ever have to be sorry to me. Neither does your brother, even if he is a bloody arrogant know-it-all. I just ask you one favour.'

'Sure,' he whispered.

'You and I have always had an understanding. It's why I know when to leave you be and when to step in. I believe that's a two-way street. I would hate to ever lose that. I just ask that you be the one person who doesn't think he knows me better than I know myself.'

Simon simply stared, defeated by his mother's plea. His face brightened, the dark stubble possibly hiding the crimson of his embarrassment.

Gulping back the last of the coffee, Connie slid off the chair and turned away. 'If I don't see you when you get back from the airport, please come on Sunday. I enjoyed the coffee, but I would enjoy us having an afternoon together more. Tell Gordon to have a safe flight and we'll see him on Sunday too.'

*

Ellie's world had spiraled into chaos, her mind consumed by a maelstrom of fear and confusion. Locking herself inside the house, she sought refuge within its familiar walls, but the very familiarity now felt suffocating, like she was trapped in a maze of her own torment.

She paced back and forth. Maybe there was nothing to remember. Perhaps she was torturing herself for no reason. It wasn't as if she was unhappy that someone had finally ridden her of that noose round her neck. Perhaps she wouldn't have wished that kind of death on him, but she knew he felt not an iota of cold remorse for her when he was slamming his fist into her face or pushing her to the floor.

The whispers of doubt continued to grow until they were no longer whispers but fully formed screams inside her head. The rumours of multiple stab wounds circulated, but the truth remained elusive, a haunting specter lurking in the shadows.

Ellie tore through the house, her hands ripping through drawers, overturning furniture, and shattering everything breakable in her path. She needed answers. Maybe the murder weapon was gone but the memories were locked back there somewhere and just awaiting the arrival of the key.

She couldn't get Chris fully out of her mind either. Should she warn Connie? Wouldn't that be the loyal thing to do but she knew the twentieth anniversary of Lara's death, and her thirty-eighth birthday loomed, and she didn't want to cause any more upset. She also remembered the last threat from Tommy. Did she really want to open that particular can?

As the frustration and desperation reached a crescendo, Ellie sank against the wall, her body trembling with anguish. Tears streamed down her face as she clung to the remnants of her imploding existence.

CHAPTER SEVENTEEN

Rainie McDermott stormed past the yellow tape surrounding the crime scene, her unsteady steps revealing her intoxicated state. She swiftly approached the door of the chapel house. Father Brady, expecting her to inquire about funeral arrangements, opened the door with a solemn expression.

'I need to speak to you, Bill,' she roared, words slurred as she pushed past.

He closed the door. 'Now might not be the best time to discuss funeral arrangements, Lorraine. Let's get you a coffee.'

'I'm not here about funeral arrangements,' she boomed. 'That bastard doesn't deserve a funeral. Throw him in the lake. That's what he deserves.'

The priest tried to maintain his composure, conceal his shock in fact as he opened the dining room and escorted her in.

It was a large rectangular room that outsiders might have expected to be either barren of personality or a shrine to God himself. Instead, it was modern and bright, adorned with paintings that Father Brady had committed to canvas himself. He perched on the edge of a chair at the end of a twelve-person dining table, dark oak and scarred by the passage of time, the only nod to anything aged in the room.

Her eyes narrowed, searching Father Brady's face for answers. 'Did you know? Did you know what he had done?'

Father Brady's gentle voice carried a hint of sadness. 'No, Rainie. I didn't know.'

She shook her head vehemently, the alcohol fueling her emotions. 'You've known him fifty years. Your confessional was practically his bloody office.'

'That's not the case. In fact, Max may well have known my thoughts on some of his business affairs and therefore not shared them with me.'

'He trusted you more than anyone else in the world.'

'With his soul, perhaps,' iterated the priest, shifting uncomfortably on his chair. He could see the venom in her expression, the urge to anger. 'Not his business dealings. He spoke to me very little about those.'

'Well, this wasn't a business dealing. Are you telling me you haven't seen it?'

Father Brady adjusted the spectacles on the bridge of his nose as she pulled out her mobile phone and fumbled with the screen. He waited with extraordinary patience as she tried to find what she was looking for.

'This,' she screamed, thrusting the phone so hard that it almost reached his face.

Father Brady recoiled, watched ten seconds of the moving images, and then turned away in silent disgust. 'I have now knowledge of that,' 'he stated, matter-of-factly and avoiding any hint of expression in his tone.

'Liar,' she hissed.

'I'll remind you this is a house of God. My house. I realise your upset but please keep it civil.' It wasn't often that Bill Brady was moved to reaction but the video itself had unsettled him and Rainie's behaviour troubled him. 'I did not know anything about this, and it is not something the chapel either condones or condemns.' The words felt alien as he spoke them. How could he not judge? It revolted him. The girl in that video was barely more than a child. Max himself looked younger than now but it must have still had him in his late forties or early fifties.

She stood, forcing the handset back into her tight jean pocket. There had been an attempt for her to mount her highlighted hair into a loose bun but some of it had fallen out and her face had been aged by a grief she did not want to admit to. Perhaps she wasn't in grief for her husband's loss of life but for the loss of truth in a marriage that had lasted almost four decades. 'All boys stick together,' she droned.

In a rare moment of recourse, Father Brady put his hand on her shoulder. 'Lorraine, if you did not know what was happening in your own house, can you really blame other people when they tell you they don't know. This,' he pointed at her pocket, 'is on no-one but Max himself. He will be the person who faces judgement at the gates of heaven. All we can do is pray for his soul.'

She moved back to the door, stumbling slightly as she found her balance. She turned to him. 'I will never pray for his soul. I hope his skin is already melted onto his bones in hell.'

He sighed and looked out the window. As he squinted, he saw a figure standing in the distance. They weren't part of the crime scene and didn't appear to be searching periphery for clues. Instead, they stood, a vaguely familiar silhouette concealed by the afternoon sun.

Father Brady moved to the window and saw Rainie storm down the pathway, past the church until she was no longer in sight. He looked across the landscape of the cemetery once more, just in time to see the red hood disappear into the trees.

*

As the door swung open, revealing a figure standing before her, Ellie's heart lurched forwards. Had Connie passed on her suspicions after all? Was this how life would go for her now, constantly searching the faces of those she knew for an indication they suspected her of murder?

It should have been a relief to find Richie standing on the doorstep. In the same way that Connie had treated her like a daughter, so had Richie. Not in an absurd, untoward way but as if she had always been part of the family even when Lara was alive. Instead, she found herself back in a vortex of suspicion and guilt. She searched his face just before he leaned in to give her a tight hug. Could it be him?

'How are the horses?'

He spoke in hushed tones, like no-one should hear but that was Richie, the picture of discretion and always the gentlest of men. 'They're distressed. We've had to move them to other places but they're safe and we didn't lose any.'

She smarted because it was just one more thing she suspected Chris of being guilty of. Why, though? He had shown her the screen for the rest of his masterplan, but she hadn't seen anything obvious about burning down the stables. Anything was possible, though she wouldn't say yet. She felt conflicted between those she had always known and a man she knew to be innocent of such heinous accusations.

'How are you bearing up, kid?'

She shrugged, aware now that Connie probably hadn't said anything about the subtle implications of their earlier conversation. 'Better than you might think.'

'Why didn't you tell me what he was doing to you? I could have helped.'

'Oh, you know about that,' she said. 'Listen, every marriage has their problems.'

Richie laughed, a rare moment of relief in an endless melee. 'Yes, they do. I can't tell you the times I've had to bite down on my hand to avoid a confrontation. Connie is an absolute witch at her worst. Some men might have left years ago but I know the other Connie that lives under her skin. The same woman who would protect us with everything in her. Same as she would do for you. Never, though, in all those years of her mood swings and then her menopausal rages, would I ever have hit her.'

The fact she had been abused was now common knowledge. She would never be the old Ellie, pre-marriage, pre-kids, or pre-abuse again. The narrative she wanted to take back now that Tommy was gone would forever be intertwined with the perception that she was a victim.

Ellie had never wanted to be a victim.

Could that be the reason she might have lashed out? Maybe she grabbed something sharp and dug it deep into his flesh. Ellie was at the head of her own suspect list but then she couldn't remember much about the night before. Nor could she remember being at the cemetery. Had she met Tommy there? Maybe he'd followed her somewhere. The memory evaded her, but she still couldn't shake the feeling that something had happened between them.

Richie grabbed her hand. 'Why don't you come and stay at ours. There's plenty of room and the boys are all coming over at the weekend. Go and get the kids and we'll all just sit round the table and eat.'

She drew her hand away, softly enough that it didn't look like she was snatching it away or rejecting his kindness. 'I'm hoping to be gone by then, Richie. I can't stay here. Not now. Even with Tommy gone, everybody will know what he did.'

Another glance and she noticed him dip his eyes quickly to evade meeting with her gaze. It could be you, she thought. Was Richie capable of harming anyone? He didn't kill for his own daughter, why would he kill for her?

A wall of silence fell between them, the shades down on the conversation. She couldn't stop thinking about Chris. She had run from him but in those moments it had all become too much. The death of Max McDermott, the arrest of Darren and the death of Tommy all seemingly interconnected but with one basic hole in the boat. Chris had willingly taken responsibility for what had happened to Max and Darren, but he was vehement that he had not been near Tommy. Could she trust him? Could she trust anyone? Ellie feared she couldn't even trust herself.

'Remember the offer's there,' said Richie, breaking the silence as he stood. He moved through the small lounge and into the hallway as she followed. He opened the door just in time for the arrival of Maggie Bradley and the suited detective.

'Richie, how are you? I heard about the stables. Everybody okay?'

Ellie saw him exchange a pleasantry and a thank you, touch the policewoman's arm gently and then head to his car.

It was Maggie who spoke then, stepping in front of the awkward detective who had escorted Ellie to the chapel house earlier. 'Ellie, darling. Can we come in? We just have some questions about Tommy.'

Ellie stood back and allowed them passage into the house. Then, catching the prying eye of a curious neighbour across the street, she closed the door and blocked out any unwanted intrusion.

CHAPTER EIGHTEEN

Chris sat in the quiet solitude of his loft; his mind consumed with the events of the past few days. With every passing moment he felt just a little guiltier because Ellie had expressed her disdain and fear by running. Running from him, in fact. Just as he suspected Lara might have done if she had been here to learn of his actions.

He blocked his eyeline with the binoculars and searched the backward hills for signs of life. Sign perhaps that the Gibbs were home and unaware how mercilessly their lives were about to be destroyed. Chris didn't know how yet because he hadn't worked out the finer details. In the cataclysm of rat-bastard behaviour, the Gibbs had managed to stay squeaky clean.

He thought of Ellie's place in that family, the poor stepsister essentially, and he questioned once more what he'd seen when she leaned into Richie's car. Had it been so innocent? Was he searching the realms of darkness for something that simply wasn't there?

Chris wasn't thinking straight. He needed help. He wanted this over with sooner rather than later, but he'd come too far to give up now. So, he scrolled through his contacts until he came to an old friend in Glasgow. Sammy Winters was the one person he had always been able to trust. Years could go by with no contact, but both would dance through a dragon's fire for the other.

The ringing echoed in his ears until the call connected, and Chris could hear the familiar voice of his old friend on the other end.

'Sammy, mate. How are you? It's Chris.'

'Yeah, I know, Chris. Your number comes up on my screen. How are you, pal?'

'I'll cut straight through the crap, Sam. I need help,' Chris said, his voice tinged with urgency.

There was a moment of silence, and then Sammy's voice crackled through the phone. 'What do you need?'

Chris hesitated for a moment, torn by his thoughts of Tommy Hunter's death or his own path of vengeance. This was the final part of his masterpiece. The great fall of the high and mighty. In the end, though, there was no clever plot, no device that would serve them up on a platter. It would just be him versus them. As it had been from the day he'd laid eyes on Lara.

Richie had never deemed him good enough for his daughter. He'd worked the summers up at the stables before meeting Lara and hadn't even remembered her the first night she walked into a bar in Callander. She had taken his breath away from that moment on.

He imagined Lara now. Would she still be as vibrant and beautiful? It was hard to imagine her at this age, or anything like poor worn emaciated Ellie. He could almost feel her breath on his neck as he paused momentarily. She would never have approved. Even in her worst moments with her family, Lara adored her mother and father, and she thought her two younger brother's walked on golden clouds. Then again, she didn't live to learn the true nature of her vindictive parents.

'I'm at my mother's house. Did you see the news about Max McDermott, that infamous lawyer from up here?'

'I knew McDermott in a past life. He tried to get a conviction on me a few years ago. Can't say it happened to a nicer guy.'

'It was me,' said Chris, after a lengthy question mark. 'I sent the details to his wife and to the rest of the village.'

Sammy didn't speak at first. 'What the fuck, Chris? Where do you even come across that kind of shit?'

'Not willingly, put it that way. I needed to do it. They destroyed my life, cut me off from my mother and they were instrumental in her suicide. I'll never forgive or forget.' He placed the binoculars down on the old scabby table and moved to the hatch.

'Is this about Lara?'

'In part,' confessed Chris. 'In part it is about taking back what's mine. I'm selling my mother's house but not before I wreck their lives like they did mine.'

'What do you need?'

In that moment as he stared down the hatch, Chris suddenly saw a shadow shift on the ground floor. Someone was inside his house. He paused, caught his breath, and contemplated what he would need for the final act of his plan.

'Chris? What do you need?' Sammy sounded more persistent now.

'Hang on,' he said, stepping back just enough that whoever lurked down there wouldn't see him easily. Just as he couldn't see them easily. He waited in silence, suddenly fearful that someone had been watching him during his time here. He pressed the phone to his chest and moved forward.

The figure on the ground floor, a flurry of shadows turned and ran. There was an almighty clatter as something crashed to the ground.

Chris slid down the loft stairs and then pressed against the banister of the steps to the ground floor. By the time he got to the ground floor he could already see that the back door was swinging to a close. He continued onwards, determined to find out who had been lurking in his house. His breathing had quickened, his heart stumbling over the occasional missed beat. He wasn't a frightened man, but Chris always liked to know what he was facing.

He stepped outside, saw his car was still beneath the viaduct where he had been keeping it. He looked round, nothing to see. The person who had been in his house was gone or, at the very least, hiding somewhere beyond the house.

He took a moment to compose himself then he pressed the handset back to his ear. 'Sorry, just thought I saw a ghost.' He paused for a moment, wondering which of the many ghosts it might have been. 'Okay, so listen, I need something from you. Something untraceable. Do you think you can help?'

Sammy laughed softly. 'I can always help you, but I don't know that I'd really be helping you if that makes any sense. Best you just spit it out and I'll say yay or nay.'

Chris sounded it out in his own mind, aware of the silliness. 'Okay, I need a shooter, but it can't be registered and Sammy,' he paused momentarily. 'It cannot be linked to anyone involved in any other crimes.

*

As Ellie settled into her chair in the corner of the room, she placed herself deliberately where she could sit in a strip of darkness. She didn't want to be seen. Not by them because she feared they had the same doubt in her innocence as she did.

Ellie didn't really know Detective Ryan Starling. He was new to the local force, but she had seen him round. He was stern, what her aunt would have described as pinch faced. Though, now, he seemed kind and sensitive. A ploy to get her to open up, she mused.

'Firstly, I want to say we're very sorry about the loss of your husband. It won't be an easy time and it can't help to have us intruding. We'll try and get all the information we need and get out of your way as quickly as possible. I also want to say we have appointed you a family liaison officer to help you through this tragic time.'

'That won't be necessary,' said Ellie, panicking

because she knew someone else in her home would only add another layer to her anxiety. 'The kids are in Edinburgh. They won't be returning and as soon as this is all over, I'll be packing up my things and selling the house.'

Maggie frowned. 'Ellie, this is not a time to make decisions like that. You've only just found out your husband was murdered.'

Seeing Maggie's immediate concern, Ellie realised she had overshared. Tommy was dead less than a day and she had already announced her plans to sell up and run. She decided it would be best to run with half a truth than a full lie. 'I had already planned to leave. That's why Cole is in Edinburgh with Elizabeth. We were getting away from Tommy and from here.'

Ryan, clearly a seasoned performer, pounced. 'Ellie, can you explain the current status of your marriage to Mr. Hunter?'

In her mind, she was wearing the mantle of black widow with pride. She might have said, *'Well I would have thought it obvious, I'm alive, he's dead.'* Ellie wasn't that brash, nor brave. 'We were going through a split. It wasn't a split he was happy about, but the truth is, our marriage was never a good one.'

'Was there a reason for that?' He leaned forward, urging Maggie to write the notes with a roll of the hand.

'No, not really.' A momentary ray of light passed over her face.

His lip upturned at one side, half smile, half cynical smirk. 'Our station arrested Mr. Hunter for domestic abuse twice, both in response to nine-nine-nine calls from you. Was that the only time he lifted a hand to you?'

Ellie eyed Maggie's face which was etched deep with concern. Maggie would undoubtedly know what the truth was. Was there any point fabricating her life now? A knot of dread twisted in her gut because however cold and unfeeling she was appearing; she didn't want to give them ammunition to arrest her. Not when she didn't even know if she had committed the act herself.

'You can tell us, Ellie. We're not here to catch

you out,' said Maggie.

'That's exactly why you're here,' thought Ellie, but didn't verbalise it. 'It's no secret that Tommy was violent. Not just to me but to others who were too frightened to press charges. He had a volatile nature. Even when we were children. Truth is, he didn't ever want to marry me. I was the consolation prize.'

Maggie moved up the sofa and reached for Ellie's hand. 'Absolutely not. He was lucky to have you, Ellie.'

Ellie turned away, suddenly feeling herself ready to weep but wondering why. Was it a sadness for herself, the realisation that she had always played second fiddle to the vibrant and vivacious best friend for the first half of her life, spending the second half locked inside the hollow shadow of a ghost?

'He wanted Lara. He couldn't take his eyes off her. Even after she chose Chris Burns and I agreed to be with him, he was so enraged that someone would have the audacity to not want him that it resulted in many fights.'

'Between you two?'

She snorted, managing just in time to swallow back salty tears. 'Between us, between them, between anyone who got in his way. I'm surprised you only have two arrests on his charge sheet because he spent more of his life brawling than he ever did being a husband or a father.' The words were tumbling out and she knew she should have regretted them. The bitterness encased every syllable. She didn't because she finally had a forum for twenty years of hurt and betrayal and it felt good. Still, she was aware not to say too much.

'There was another charge,' interrupted Ryan. 'A drug smuggling charge.'

'What? No, that can't be. He never did a single day in prison in his life.'

Ryan nodded. 'Exactly, but it happened. He was arrested for trying to pass illegal substances through Glasgow International Airport.'

She couldn't conceal her shock. Ellie didn't know how Tommy supported himself. He took from her mostly and contributed nothing to the upkeep of his children. It was his absolute entitlement to take the crumbs from Ellie's table, or so he believed. However, she did know he sometimes involved himself in things that he shouldn't. She had never worried for the day to the police turned up to arrest him, she waited with baited breath.

'What was his relationship to Max McDermott?'

Another bolt of shock rippled through her. 'Nothing. Max McDermott wouldn't shine his shoes in this part of the village. Why?'

'It was he who got Tommy out of the cells when he was arrested for assaulting you. More bizarrely though, he marched Tommy out of the holding cells at the airport without a charge to his name. A man like that doesn't do favours for people like Tommy. Does he?'

Ellie shook her head. 'If he ever did, it never made it into my bank account. We lived on fresh air for years round here because Tommy spent his money on women, drink and whatever else he fancied.'

'Drugs?'

She shrugged. Genuinely, she didn't know what her husband had been involved in and certainly didn't know if he was drunk or high when he lashed out at her. 'Not that I ever saw. That doesn't mean no.'

As the conversation continued, Maggie stepped in with a question of her own. 'I suspect Tommy assaulted you more than twice, Ellie? Why has it taken you this long to decide to leave him?'

'Fear,' she said, shocked herself that she would make such a brazen assertion and with such confidence. Had Tommy really had such a hold on her that his death would give her this turn of confidence. 'When the person who should love you the most tells you you're unattractive, it doesn't take long for that to become a fact. When a person beats you for not having the baked beans at the right temperature, you learn to make sure they're at the right temperature and not complain when he decides to beat you for not putting just the right amount on the plate.'

She searched for judgement on both Ryan and Maggie's face, but she didn't find it and that almost made the shame return in floods.

Ryan stepped in once more. 'Did your husband

ever hit your children.'

'No,' she said. 'I know I should tell you he did because they would have been his next target. It all fell on me. I took the beatings and honestly, if he had touched them, you might have found his body years ago.'

'Did you kill your husband?'

Ellie didn't know what to say. She could feel his eyes, wide with anticipation burning on to her like someone branding her with a soldering iron. She didn't know. That was the truth. She had a list of suspects in her mind and she, herself stood at the top of it. 'No, I was asleep all night.'

She dipped her eyes because she didn't care what Ryan though of her, but Maggie had been someone she had known her entire life. She had babysat Maggie's boys as young children when she was in her teens. She had even taken Tommy there a few times. She didn't dare challenge Maggie to search behind her eyes because she wasn't sure either would like what they saw.

When she looked up, she saw that Detective

Starling was already on his feet.

'Ellie are you sure you don't want my colleague to come and help you. They can be with you when you see your children or when you need to start arrangements.'

'Arrangements?'

'His funeral. Once the postmortem results are in and we're able to release his remains to you, you'll perhaps need support then. There may also be press intrusion, especially if it gets out there that there were domestic issues.'

'I don't want anyone,' said Ellie. 'It'll be a quiet funeral, a dignified affair because whatever happened between us, he was still my husband and I owe him that.' Words that belied how she really felt.

Maggie suddenly grabbed her hand and eyeballed her. 'If you or the kids need anything, you just call. You may not want official police with you but that doesn't mean I can't be a friend.'

Would you be offering if you knew I might have done it, wondered Ellie? She escorted them both to the door, thinking where she might have hidden the potential murder weapon. Once they were gone, she pressed her back against the door and allowed a silent scream to penetrate her body. Then, a sudden thought occurring to her, she ran to the kitchen and searched the cupboard for the knife block that she kept hidden there. It was true. One very large slot lay empty. The biggest knife in the block was missing and it only further confounded her belief that she didn't have to look far to find Tommy's killer. She took the block out, searched the kitchen for some bubble wrap and then sealed it inside a bag. It was inevitable the police would be back to search the house eventually. She couldn't risk that they would find a knife block with a missing blade.

Ten minutes later, Ellie stood on the pier and threw the bag into the lake and watched it disappear from the surface.

*

Maggie found Ryan sitting in the evidence room eyeing the screen. 'Anything making sense yet?'

He shook his head. 'There wasn't much love for this guy, based on what everyone around the village has said so far. I've just a call from forensics saying that the DNA in a hair sample found in his blood belongs to Ellie but it goes for nothing. That could have been a holdover from when he last seen her.'

'Or it could be vital. Are you going to follow up?'

'Yes,' he said, pushing the information around a little. 'This should be so simple but honestly, the impression I'm getting is that it could be anyone.'

'Maybe it was,' she said, gleefully calling to mind her love of Agatha Christie. 'Maybe everyone had a go.'

'No,' he said, 'this was personal and if it wasn't his wife then I believe it was someone acting on her behalf.'

Maggie looked at him with disbelief. 'I doubt it.'

He smirked, knowingly. 'She may not have asked for the help but what if someone decided to give her it anyway.'

He left it hanging in the air and then walked back out the door leaving Maggie to ponder over a mental tick list of potential suspects.

CHAPTER NINETEEN

Richie's footsteps echoed as he approached Drew's house, knowing his son would be out. It was a time for a family to be together after what had happened at the stables, and he had deliberately sent Drew to the next town to collect food for tonight's barbecue. He needed to see Stephanie alone.

He reached the front door, took a deep breath, and then rang the doorbell.

The door swung open, and Stephanie stood with a warm smile. 'Richie, it's been a long time,' she mocked.

'I know. I just wanted to come by and see my boy. Is he awake?'

'He's in the living room. Drew's not home though.'

'I know,' admitted Richie. 'I asked him if he would mind grabbing some more burgers. We've barbecued ourselves into bankruptcy this week.'

She laughed. 'You should have said, we would have got some supplies in. You and Connie are always so generous to pay for everything.'

Not anymore, thought Richie. He sat down on the floor where Oliver was biting on a bear. 'Hey little guy, how's papa's boy?' He lifted Oliver into his lap and tugged gently on the blonde curl at the front of the child's head.

Oliver rocked slightly, then let out a squeal of approval.

'Stephanie, can I ask you something?'

'Of course, Richie,' she replied, amicable as ever.

'Were the stables having financial difficulty?'

She moved to sit beside him, an expression of worry spreading across her face. 'Why? You aren't worried that Drew is involved in the fire because he would never do that.'

'I know. I'm just making sure everything checks out. The investigators will be like preying-mantis' swooping all over my land trying to find something so the insurance company can get away with not paying out. I don't want to give them any reason to doubt. I don't check the books as you know. I leave all of that to Drew and I trust him but right now, I'm not sure I trust anybody.'

'I understand,' she said. 'He was up in the early hours of the morning after the fire went out just trying to keep the workers calm and assure them there is still a job for them. I'm just glad the horses are all right.'

Richie trusted his children. There was never a moment in their lives where they'd let him down. Other people, perhaps, but his family always stepped up when they needed. He was proud of those boys, each in their own way. However, he knew Drew could be hot-headed and sometimes acted rash in difficult situations.

Stephanie, clearly sensing his concern, leaned towards him and rubbed his shoulder. 'You have nothing to worry about. Drew takes great care of those horses and as far as I know, the stables have been going great guns since everything re-opened.'

Drew knew she was telling the truth and that he had no reason to doubt Drew but that made it all the more worrying. He put Oliver back on the play mat and moved to the sofa beside Stephanie. 'That's a relief,' he said, solemnly.

'But what?'

He shrugged. 'If it wasn't insurance related, and it wasn't an act of God then it means it was a deliberate act of vandalism. Someone let our horses out and then burned it to the ground. That's more than just foul play,' he continued. 'That's an act of aggression.'

'By whom though?'

He looked at Stephanie. 'Isn't it strange that it happened on the same day that one of my oldest friends was driven to suicide by something in his past and that another friend has been arrested for corruption.'

Her eyes widened, a slight tremor settling on her lip. 'Why would someone target the stables, or you for that matter?'

He stood to leave, his mind swirling with an amalgamation of questions but absolutely no answers. 'That's exactly what I intend to find out.'

*

Ellie dialed Elizabeth's number, conflicted by the

terror of the news she was about to share and the excitement of telling her children she would be joining them and never have to worry about Tommy again. She feared that Cole would not see it that way, and she understood it. His father was still his father, after all. The phone rang, each moment stretching like an eternity, until finally, Elizabeth's voice filled the air.

'Why have you taken this long to call me to tell me my father's dead?'

Ellie was taken aback at first and then she grew angry. Someone had evidently put the information out there and she hadn't had a chance to tell her kids what had happened. 'I'm sorry, Elizabeth,' she said. 'It's been a crazy day. If I explain everything to you then you might understand that I haven't acted in the way I should.'

'Did you kill him?'

'No,' shrieked Ellie. 'God, why does everyone keep assuming that?' She buried the nagging guilt and tightened her eyes under the heavy burden of the lie. If it was a lie. She didn't know.

She listened to the water drip across the kitchen as silence created a short divide. Finally, she broke it. 'I don't want either of you to worry. I did not kill your father, but the police are going to find out whoever did and when they do, we'll all be able to move on from this awful place.'

CHAPTER TWENTY

Ryan sat in his small office at the police station, surrounded by a clutter of papers filled with hastily scribbled notes. His lanky frame was hunched over the desk, and his fingers tapped anxiously on the surface. He had been casting an eye over the details of Tommy's death, no closer to having any real insight.

The clock on the wall ticked away, the sound punctuating the silence of the room. Ryan glanced at it periodically, aware that every second was precious time lost. Patience might have been a virtue, but it wasn't one he'd been gifted with.

Ryan didn't believe Ellie had killed Tommy but there was something about her cold demeanour that made him uneasy. There was also the strand of her hair found in his blood. She didn't strike him as a woman who was frightened but then maybe she had nothing to fear now that the man who instilled that fear was no longer a threat.

Seventeen stab wounds though. That was

frenzied by any standard. He just couldn't relax until forensics came back with more information. He was reminded in that instant of his mother's silly old quip that a watched kettle didn't boil.

Theories formed then dissipated like fleeting shadows. Scenarios danced across his head, but they only served to muddy the waters. With a sigh, Ryan leaned back in his creaking chair, his fingers laced behind his head. He closed his eyes for a moment, feeling his way mentally across the blank tapestry that hadn't even begun to weave together.

Ryan prided himself on working his best when he was allowed to disappear into his own little world. He often sought solace behind his eyelids, quiet reflection allowing his mind the space to breathe. Inner chaos didn't faze him. It was the external forces of the vast big world that burdened him.

He sat there, senses sharpened, muffled conversations in the distance. He could hear the clatter of equipment and the occasional phone ringing. The rhythmic hum of the air conditioning was both comforting and irritating as it cooled but whirred in his ear.

Averting his eyes, Ryan's gaze fell upon a photograph of Tommy Hunter. The image captured a vibrant young man with a mischievous smile frozen in time. It was an old photo, a de-aged teen with the world at his feet. Of course, there was another photo that showed how that world had not been kind to him, nor him to it.

Ryan began jotting down his thoughts, organising the details, and drawing connections. The act of writing helped him regain focus, channeling his restless energy into something productive. He moved to the window, saw the sun reach its zenith and realised there was only a few hours of daylight. He grabbed his jacket; glad Maggie had gone home for now. He needed the head space to investigate without leading the horse to water. Once he was able to stand back and see all the dots, they might join just a little easier. After all, this village had suddenly become a hub of dramatic events in the past two days. He likened it to one of those magic eye pictures he loved as a child. Once he looked at it all from a different angle, things might just start to become clearer.

*

The evening news was framed by the news of Max McDermott's death. *Tragic suicide*, screamed the headlines with no regard for anything remotely close to the truth.

Ellie sat on her sofa with a hot water bottle pressed against her tummy because the stress of the day had thrown her into a flare up of irritable bowel syndrome. She had lit a Parma violet scented candle and rather enjoyed the orange hue spreading up the wall, licking at the cornice along the edge of the ceiling.

Outside the wind cried. Rain tricked, the threat of a summer storm to wash away the heat.

She hadn't known anything about Tommy's dealings or that he had any contact with Max. How odd that she only learned of it when both men died. Could Tommy have been involved in the sordid doings with Max? She tried not to think of it because living with an abuser was bad enough without learning he was capable of what max was being accused of.

It made her think of Darren Philips. Then Chris. Didn't she owe Chris an apology for running off on him? She has been taken aback by his presence not to mention the suspicion that he might have committed murder for her. Why not? He was responsible for someone else's death. Yet she could not bring herself to go to that place. Not after he'd lived under the murky depths of such an accusation once before.

Something glinted.

She hadn't noticed it before. It was there now though. Something shiny that caused a sharp inhalation of breath.

Ellie stood. She crossed the room and gasped. Grabbing onto the cold radiator, Ellie lowered herself down, feeling the ache as her stomach folded into her upper thighs. She reached inwards and jacked the sharp blade out from behind the radiator. It thudded onto the floor, the dried blood instantly sending a surge through her entire body. In that moment, the suspicion that she had killed Tommy gathered credibility and she found herself throwing some last garments into her suitcase with the urge upon her to run as far and as quickly as she could.

*

''I can't just go in there and ask for his number.'

Lara stood outside the bar, adjusted the strap on her micro-top and hitched her skirt just enough that a little more of her long legs were revealed.

Ellie laughed. Just as she always did right before Lara got them into some sort of bother.

'Of course, you can. Poor Sister Ellie. Honestly, I don't know why you don't take your holy orders. Come on, lets live a little before I get so old that my mother is more fun than we are.'

'Your mother is Connie Gibbs. She IS more fun than we are.'

'Only because you want to be her. Wait until she's trying to turn you into her and then you might not find it so enticing.' She applied another layer of dark lipstick and fixed her breasts in the window reflection. Then, she walked away.

'I wouldn't mind being Connie,' said Ellie, reflecting sadly on her own other self, seeing her own

lanky reflection, flat hair, colourless skin and baggy shirt hanging limply on her protruding bones.

'What?'

'Nothing,' said Ellie, following Lara into the bar and hoping that she wasn't going to play second fiddle to her best friend, as usual.

Chris Burns and Tommy Hunter were already playing a game of pool. They instantly looked up as Lara made her entrance. She swooped over, her swagger contradicting her mere sixteen years of life. That was Lara, full of energy and bustling with a confidence that only came from growing up in a house where everybody treated you like Queen of the world.

'Hey, girls. Are you sure you're old enough to be in here?' said Tommy, clearly trying to impress his friend and failing miserably.

Lara grabbed the white ball from the table and threw herself up into a sitting position on the edge. 'Chris knows how old I am, don't you Chris? He's one of my dad's hands. Is his say-so good enough for you, dickhead?'

He blushed, his eyes blazing.

She moved towards him and licked her lips. 'Are you going to search me for ID or buy me a drink?'

She didn't need to ask Tommy twice; he was already on his way to the bar without asking Ellie what she would like.

'How are you?'

Chris was gentler than his friend, also more respectful and he made Ellie feel like it was okay to be there without treating her like the third wheel on a hitched wagon. It was evident though, to anyone with eyes that here lay the moment where Chris and Lara fell in love. Their young untarnished eyes fell into each other, the start of a love that should have lasted a lifetime but was hastily halted by fate.

Ellie didn't know that yet, but she knew envy when it burned deep in her heart. She looked at Lara, stepping onto her platform and commanding the attention of every young man in the vicinity.

Meanwhile, Ellie would stay in the shadow of her beautiful, vibrant best friend, loving her with the same tenacity that she had always envied her with.

One day she'd wish to be that envious again.

CHAPTER TWENTY-ONE

Simon

The broad strokes came heavier by the minute. As he stood by the window up on the top floor room of his town house, Simon pushed heavily onto the canvas and bit down hard on his lower lip. The blurred lines he had painted hadn't formed much of an image, but they were an amalgamation of the still waters waiting to implode within him.

He thought of the conversation with his mother yesterday and Simon realised she was right. People who didn't understand always tried to fix. People who thought they knew better always patronized. He and Connie were two of the same breed and that's why they connected deep beneath the surface.

Gordon was gone for the next few days. He loved Gordon but at this time in his life, Simon was glad of the space. It had become a lot recently particularly with the other things going on in the village.

He laid the brush on the easel and moved to the window. There was nothing much to see on the streets of Crianlarich at this early hour of the day because many people would be working, either from home or they'd already be at work. So, that left Simon in this solitude that had become both a haven and a bleak cavern for him.

He did love this view though. In one direction he could see the houses that bordered the village as well as the ones on the mounting peaks. On the other side, he stared onto the lake, a place of calming peace sometimes and aching loss at others. How beautiful it was. How dangerously treacherous it could be.

Something else was on Simon's mind though as he retrieved the tiny brush and continued to dab at the edges of the forming image. It began to take shape. First the eye, creased by age and drooping in anger, then a set of flared nostrils. A mouth came next, tucked up at the corner with a slight dimple that detracted from the age of the eyes. In the background, a medley of red and black, possibly the colours of the soul.

Simon picked up a cooling mug that he'd brought to his upstairs studio with him. Then, he looked out the window again. This time he caught sight of himself, his face adorned with carefully manicured stubble, bronzed skin glowing in the soft light of another late summer morning, and eyes that shimmered with a hint of Celtic mystery that he inherited from his father, Richie.

His mind wandered, the focus on the painting drifting and he found himself staring into the dark empty windows of the house across the street. They were the oldest cottages, more than one hundred and fifty years old, and carried the majority of the village's history within their walls. That wasn't what ailed him though because Simon had a secret. Something he hadn't shared with anyone. He lined another stroke, this time curling a deep orange from the chin of the man in the painting, and he began to recognise him.

He thought of Tommy. Once upon a time he had been so impressed by Tommy. He'd revealed his love to the man over beers one night and Tommy had taken him in his arms and danced with him. It had been a moment of revelation because it was then Simon knew where his path was leading. He'd never forgotten that moment of kindness because few saw it in Tommy. Its why Simon had cried so recklessly when he learned of Tommy's death. He wondered, just as Ellie had in the passing hours, who might have been responsible. There was only one person Simon could think of.

He looked once more at the growing splatter of black and red and the face that had already set in the midst of it all. The man who had brought so much destruction and pain to their lives. No longer able to look at the painting, Simon stormed away and pulled a hooded top over his head. He had somewhere to be. He had no idea where yet, but he knew that when he began to tail Chris Burns, just as he had the day before, he would be led to whatever trouble the man had brewed for them.

Simon sensed the reckoning was coming but whose reckoning would it be? He had to protect his family. At thirteen years old he hadn't been able to save his sister and Chris had been absent in the subsequent years. As the darkness of that fateful night plagued him, Simon knew he would do whatever it took to protect Connie and Richie. Even if meant he had to kill Chris with his bare gentle hands.

CHAPTER TWENTY-TWO

Shame was not new to Ellie. She had lived most of her life in a labyrinth of humiliation, but this felt different. She had come to the realisation when she held the knife in her hand that she must be the perpetrator of her husband's death. Maybe that's why she felt so cold towards it. Maybe connecting with it meant she had to admit to feeling something, to still loving him despite loathing him enough to plunge an eight-inch blade into his vital organs.

In the grim cold of the blue interview room, barren of life or anything remotely resembling humanity, she suddenly found herself in the grip of panic. She had been in the path of violence for twenty years and no-one, including herself had raised an eyelid. Now, most likely guilty of one retaliation, she was about to lose everything. Ellie found herself scrambling for a possible alternative truth. Perhaps it was time to speak about the return of Chris Burns.

'Ellie, can you describe again to us your relationship with your husband, the deceased?'

She flinched at the suggestion there was any relationship at all. 'We were over. He thought it was temporary. I knew there was no coming back from that last time.'

'The last time?'

She lifted her glittery silver top to reveal a massive bruise, yellow and black merging with the skin. 'Tommy said what most men like him said; that they never aimed for the face because people saw the face. So, for me, it was my abdomen. Though, I would say this is the worst he has ever bruised that area.'

Maggie turned away in disgust but when her expression softened, she leaned forward and urged Ellie on. 'Ellie, we are going to be presenting a case for you. There's two arrests on file though I must be honest, it's flimsy compared to what we might have had if you had pressed charges and made Tommy pay for what he did. Let us help you though. Tell us what happened on the night he died.'

Ellie crossed her hands, folded her fingers into each other. 'That's the problem, I don't know.'

Ryan leaned forward so he could sit head-to-head with his colleague. 'Tell us the last thing you remember, that will let us get a picture of what might have led to Tommy's death.'

'I was at the lake,' she admitted. 'I go there often because it makes me feel better. It makes me feel closer...' Her voice trailed off.

'Was Tommy there with you?'

'Yes,' she whispered, her eyes glistening under a sheet of readily formed tears.

'Was there anyone else there with you?'

She looked at Ryan and had an instant insight into his motives. Ellie believed he was more interested in his conviction rate than he was in the truth. A dangerous notion. 'No,' she lied.

'That's not what we've been told Ellie. We've been told that someone saw him strike you and that you were pushed to the ground.'

She didn't respond, simply stared for a sympathetic eye, and quickly learned it wasn't going to happen.

'That must have made you really quite angry,' he

continued.

It had, thought Ellie, but to admit it would be to play into their hands. They could suspect anything they liked but without an admission or evidence, she was sure they'd have difficulty proving a thing. 'Not angry, just disappointed because he had promised that if I gave him one last try, he'd change. Of course, I'm not as stupid as I look. I wasn't buying it from the outset. So, yes, I would say disappointment was the feeling that came to mind.'

'Ellie, we recovered a knife block from the lake shore this morning.' Ryan pulled out the heavy evidence bag and dropped it noisily onto the table. 'There's one missing. One that most likely matches the size of the wounds inflicted on Tommy's body. Do you know anything about that?'

She flicked her hair back behind her ear and turned away. They really had overturned every stone. Except the stones they were overturning didn't belong to her and she hadn't left her mark on any of them. 'Could I have a break please? It's very warm in here and I think I need to consult a lawyer.'

Ryan stood instantly but Maggie looked a little more hesitant.

'Do you have anyone in mind?'

Ellie didn't. She had never been in trouble and if she had been, she would have asked her husband to speak to Max. The two people she would have turned about this situation were both irrevocably gone and unable to help her. She sighed in her chair as the interview was suspended and she was asked to remain in place.

Once they both left the room, Ellie's steely resolve melted. She'd never had to tough it out before, but this had been tough, no mistake. She thought of the block of knives and let out a gasp. She clearly hadn't wrapped them heavily enough but in essence, she suspected she had signed her own arrest warrant. Or maybe someone at the bottom of that lake had decided it was time for Ellie to pay.

*

Simon's heart sank as he stood on the charred remains of the stables, his eyes surveying the extent of the fire damage. The acrid scent of burnt wood lingered in the air, a testament to the destructive force that had swept through the once vibrant structure. He sidled up to Richie, still at odds to share the information about Chris, particularly in the current situation but he knew Chris was responsible for the fire. He just didn't know how he would make him pay yet.

'At least no-one was hurt, and the horses are all safe.'

Richie smiled half-heartedly. 'I love that about you, Si. You always count your blessings and I appreciate it. Unfortunately, we've a hell of a way to go before we'll get paid out and I suspect they'll be looking to paint us as insurance fraudsters. I just hope your brother has everything in order.'

Simon's heart sank. He had bailed Drew out just a few years back with a loan of ten thousand pounds. Gordon had been furious because it had been their life savings to that point. The money was paid back now, and Drew seemed to be doing well. Simon knew Drew had clawed it back, but he also knew that insurance companies would trawl through the lengthy transactions from the past and try to find a way to withhold payment. Another reason to want Chris dead.

'Drew would never do this. There are other ways if he was in trouble.'

'Such as?'

Simon was taken back by his father's cold tone. He didn't recognise it because Richie was always such a warm, inviting man. Not today. Today he looked angry, bitter, full of fury at whoever could have put his beautiful equine family at risk. Simon didn't envy anyone who got in Richie's way. Perhaps it went some way to explain why he hadn't openly declared Chris's return. He wanted to protect his father from exploding. The family had enough on their plate. No, he would handle Chris whilst his family dealt with everything else.

Drew appeared then, a rare time when the three men found themselves in the same place at the same time. He pushed into Simon, a good humoured nudge to break the tension of all that had happened. 'Not often we see you up here, little brother.'

'I wanted to come and offer some support. Is there anything I can do?'

'We just have to wait for the investigators to finish their report. I don't think there's a lot anyone can do. The horses are across three stables though, so if you find yourself at a loose end, maybe you could find your old riding gear and help us out there.'

Simon hadn't been on a horse in ten years. He'd given it up after an almighty fight with Richie about his future. Richie, of course, wanted both his sons to run the stables. Drew had been a natural. Simon had wanted to run every time he got near a horse. Of course, he loved them, but he didn't want to be on one.

'I wonder if they're any closer to finding Tommy's killer,' said Simon, momentarily changing the subject.

Drew snarled. 'Still got that little infatuation, have you? Sounds to me like he got what he deserved.'

Richie stepped between them. 'Drew, cool it.

Don't antagonize him and don't speak ill of the dead. We taught you a little decorum for god's sake.'

There was no argument from either boys because, despite his gentle nature, when Richie spoke, it silenced the room. His boys had never been lashed or hit or threatened with violence because Richie's carefully chosen words and disappointed tone had always been enough to send them crawling to their bedrooms. Whereas Connie raised them with an iron tongue.

Looking once more at the charred building, Simon felt his gut rise. He had to go now. He had showed face, wallowed a little for his family and now he was going out to ensure that no more damage happened to them.

Simon was about to say his goodbyes and turn away when his eyes locked with Drew's. There was a suspicion there. Drew's narrow left eye always gave that away. Did he think Simon had something to do with everything that had happened? How long before he had to reveal the truth? Maybe he could get rid of Chris without anyone really knowing he'd been here.

No body, no crime but he suspected Drew already sensed there was something wrong. Explanations would happen later. For now, Simon had to get back to the village in time to follow Chris to his next destination.

CHAPTER TWENTY-THREE

Ryan stood alone in the eerie stillness of the cemetery, slightly haunted by the contrast to yesterday's chaos. The morning mist had settled like a blanket over the gravestones, the soft scent of wet leaves lingering in the air. The atmosphere was thick with sorrow and an unsettling sense that there was something missing, as if the ghosts themselves now walked among the tombstones.

As he walked through the rows of graves, the detective's keen eyes scanned the ground, searching for any overlooked clues. The damp earth underfoot felt cold and unforgiving. A gust of wind rustled the leaves above him as he lifted the mobile phone in his hand and took a few snap shots. He then lowered the handset and clicked from a different angle.

And then, amid the scattered debris of fallen leaves, he spotted something that caught his attention – something he might not have noticed if it hadn't glinted beneath a sliver of sunlight. He grabbed a bag, carefully picked it up, examining the intricate design of the pendant.

He wondered if it belonged to Ellie. Perhaps it was just coincidence that it had ended up here. He wanted to believe in Ellie's innocence, but she hadn't been forthcoming, nor had she been particularly upset to learn that her husband was dead.

He searched a few more yards, tight beady eyes caressing the blades of grass. His team had missed the pendant, what else could they have missed? He didn't know if he would link the pendant to Ellie, or even to Tommy Hunter but with every moving branch and every step forward, he felt the haunting presence of a malevolent ghoul, someone snuffed out to early who had much more damage to do. As he wrestled with that thought, Ryan realised that Tommy could have made Ellie's life miserable for another fifty years. Was it really so unthinkable that she should defend herself?

He turned the corner, faced on to the chapel house and realised it was the first time in his career he had faced such a moral dilemma. In that very human moment, he felt a surge of anger towards Tommy

Hunter because he had forced Ryan into a predicament he did not relish one bit.

*

In the winding roads that snaked round Crianlarich Simon had always hated the meandering. To the outside world, those who travelled through on the West Highland Way, it was a road. They couldn't appreciate the peaks and troughs, the hidden valleys and the deep lochs that slashed through rockeries until they settled on the lake. It was divine. It was also treacherous and appeared to trapse on into infinity.

He had left the stables behind, the destruction of the fire still haunting his thoughts. As he approached his mother's shop, he stole a glance through the window, catching a glimpse of her bustling about, tending to customers with her trademark warmth. A fleeting smile crossed his lips, a silent acknowledgment of the love and strength she had instilled in him and his brother.

Yet, his attention quickly shifted, drawn to a scene unfolding by the pier. His father, Richie, stood in the company of Ellie, their figures etched against the backdrop of the lake. He had noticed how much sadder Ellie seemed. How distant and inattentive she had become; their friendship became frailer by the year. Maybe that would change now that Tommy was gone. He would never get his sister back, but he wanted his best friend back at least.

He found himself wondering why his father had met her on the pier.

He parked his car discreetly, the engine's hum fading into the background as he approached. The air crackled with an unspoken tension as he drew nearer, his presence unnoticed by his father and Ellie who were engrossed in their own world.

Simon mustered the courage to interrupt their private moment, offering his support to Ellie as he spotted the uncertainty in her face. His voice quivered with compassion as he expressed words that he knew she probably wouldn't appreciate.

Truthfully, he had long since extinguished any feeling for Tommy. He'd loved him once, secret unrequited love that had died with every violent blow he'd dealt Ellie. How could anyone love a man like that?

'I hope you aren't still thinking of leaving,' he said, bitterly. 'This is your home and he's already taken enough from you.'

'Simon,' warned his father. 'Time and place.'

Simon didn't care now. He just wanted to remind her of the deep-rooted connection she shared with his family, particularly with Lara, who had brought Ellie into their lives.

Ellie struggled to meet Simon's gaze. Her anguish, too heavy to bear, cast a shadow over the moment, obscuring any glimmer of hope that might have remained. She pushed Simon away, her sorrow pouring forth in a torrent of emotions.

'You don't understand,' Ellie choked out between sobs, her voice tinged with despair. 'I've done something... something unforgivable. I can't stay here. I know I should admit to it and face what I've done. I can't.'

Simon's heart ached as he watched Ellie crumble before him, her pain too deep to fathom. He reached out, longing to provide solace, to offer the unconditional support of people who transcended the boundaries of mere friendship. But she resisted, her anguish forming a barrier that seemed insurmountable.

'We'll protect you, won't we, dad?'

Richie nodded. 'Of course, we will, Ellie.' However, being the even measured man he was, Richie didn't finish there. 'We will also support whatever decision you make. Leaving here might be the worst mistake you make but it might also be the best thing you ever did.'

Simon felt helpless. He knew his father was trying to do what he always did, lay out the options but he resented the fact that Richie seemed not to care that they might never see Ellie or the kids again.

Ellie turned and ran without another word.

'If she leaves, dad, it'll be because she thinks we don't care.'

Richie sighed. 'Do you know, Si, sometimes I am so proud of how smart you are. Then, with something like this, I'm reminded that when it comes to people, you still don't have a clue.'

He followed Ellie off the pier, leaving Simon alone to seethe. 'No, dad, you don't have a clue,' he called after Richie, knowing he wouldn't hear him.

CHAPTER TWENTY-FOUR

Connie walked to her daughters gravestone, sick to the gut when she realised it had been part of the active crime scene. Nobody had told her Tommy's body had been discarded on her daughter's plot. Seeing now that the barrier tape had been left discarded on this very spot made her want to scream to a god she no longer trusted and would soon cease to believe in.

'Hello Connie, how are you?'

Has she been muttering to herself? She didn't know because sometimes when she was angry, she didn't realise she was doing it. She spun then, ready to lunge. 'Bill, she called out mid-way through her internal rant. 'You gave me a fright.'

He was a towering man, at least six feet tall and robust in stature. He had a calming way that even managed to settle Connie despite her defiance. 'Sorry Connie. Didn't mean to startle you. This must have been a bit of a shock to you.'

She blew into the wind. 'Yeah, about half a

minute ago. I would have thought the police might have had the decency to tell me. I thought Maggie would at least tell me.'

'I'm not defending her, but I think she might have a lot on her plate.

'My boys and her boys practically grew up together. It's a disgrace that I didn't warrant high enough on her list of priorities to tell me this. My daughter's grave has been desecrated.'

If father Brady didn't agree he certainly didn't mention it. He nodded emphatically and then moved to her side. 'Twenty years since you lost her. I wish I could unburden you of some of your pain. I can't but I believe that if you try to forgive, you can be at peace within yourself.

'Who do I forgive? The monster who caused her death? God? Myself?'

'Why do you need to forgive yourself?'

She pulled a cloth rag and bottle of water from her bag and knelt. 'I should have known he was no good. I should have warned her.'

'A mother disapproving of her daughter's choice

of boyfriend has left the world littered with warring teens and frustrated mothers. Do you think that she would listen to you had you spoken out against him? Whatever you might think of Christopher, he was her choice. She didn't go into it blindly.'

'She was sixteen when she met him,' she said, hardening her tone.

'You know it doesn't work like that.'

'I know that, but you also know how unreasonable the heart and the mind can be. No matter how many times I try to move on, I always come back here.'

He looked at the dull sky, summer finally having left its mark but finally deciding to call time. 'Then, stop.'

'Stop what?'

He frowned. 'Stop coming here, Connie. Maybe Lara doesn't need you to come here. Maybe she needs you out there,' he continued as he pointed to the village. 'Two grown up boys, a fine daughter-in-law, nice son-in-law-to-be and that little boy. You also have a marriage that has stayed solid against the odds of adversity where many wouldn't have survived. Connie, what you have in your life is such a blessing. Maybe this place isn't for you now.'

Connie felt her throat tighten, her cheeks begin to burn, and she knew she would cry. It was a conversation she'd had many times with her husband and her two sons but coming from the father, it felt authentic. Not demanding, or critical but just a soothing note from God. Perhaps his way of telling her that those mysterious motivations behind his actions served to take from those who already had too much. 'I don't think I could let her go, even if I wanted.'

Father Brady joined her at eye level. 'You will never let her go. Not coming here and torturing yourself is about preservation. About saying goodbye to the physical Lara but you'll never be forced to say goodbye to the Lara that exists in here.' He pressed on the spot that skinned her aching heart.

Connie dabbed on the stone with the damp cloth. 'This is his blood,' she said absently.

Father Brady sighed. 'Maybe you'll never be

ready,' he whispered as he stood.

Connie ignored it because she knew it to be true, but she'd lost too much time fighting for her right to be a bereaved mother. Her weapon had been her reminder to the masses that they'd never been robbed of a child they'd carried in their womb.

As Father Brady attempted to walk away, Connie called after him.

'Bill, thank you for speaking to me. You always know how to make me feel better.'

He smiled solemnly. 'I hope so.'

Connie could have followed up by telling him that at a different time, had it not been for her anger about what had taken place here with Tommy's body, his words may have penetrated. What would be the point? She suspected he would recognise the lie just as clearly as she did.

*

There was enough anonymity for Simon to pull up behind Chris through the village. Round every corner, he re-discovered nooks of the village he hadn't seen in years.

Once the village busied up, he drew breath and waited in complete silence. He saw faces he hadn't seen in a long time, accepting smiles and waves from those who knew the much younger Simon when he hadn't locked himself in this shell of a life.

He watched Chris stalk. Simon himself stalked in equal silence and with the same tenacity, though doubted he had the same malevolent plan. He let the car roll back, wondering how long before Chris would notice him. Would he recognise him?

In the dark hours of night, Simon had assessed why Chris had become such a mammoth figure in his mind, given that he himself hadn't rated high enough on Chris's list to warrant recognition. He could only attribute it to that fine line of love and hate, the one that he had crossed with Tommy. It had been more than that with Chris though. Chris had been like the big brother that he always hoped Drew would eventually become.

That's why the betrayal had cut so deep.

His thoughts shifted. Simon didn't always remember Lara. Not separately to the photographs anyway. Thirteen was a dangerous age for the memory. Things were not always as clear as a person might think. Since then, he had been driven by nostalgia and the memories fed to him by older minds. Simon remembered liking Lara very much. She was more fun and certainly, less violent towards him than Drew. However, most of his relationship with her was a tryst in dreams, a walk-through in shadows that had long since replaced any reality that might have existed.

Lara had become the ultimate unicorn, the mythical goddess that no longer existed as his sister but as a wormhole to better times.

Chris was on the move again and for one second, the sadness in Simon almost drove him to do the unthinkable. For now, he would play it safe and continue to tailgate just far behind enough that he would not lose track. The confrontation he so desired was imminent. He felt it in his angry bones. He just had to hold his breath a while longer.

CHAPTER TWENTY-FIVE

Still there was no recollection. No memory of what might have taken place. Ellie could hear the echoes of a fight that once happened. She did not know if it was from two nights ago when her husband was murdered. When she might have murdered him. It was certainly violent, but then most fights with Tommy were violent.

She lay in the holding cell, the emptiness of the space mirroring her mood. It felt like a hangover. Like one of the worst hangover's she'd ever endured. The one where she woke up the next morning, head hanging in guilt and preparing an apology for an unknown target. This wasn't a hangover though. This was pure unadulterated untapped stress, and it was rushing all the way to her head.

She mulled over and over it. Had she really been pushed this far? Why had it taken so long? She didn't care about herself, but her children would virtually be orphans if she went to prison. She had to start thinking fast. She had to get a lawyer. Someone had to fight for Ellie and her kids, and she knew it had to be her.

Ellie hoped to be out of here very soon. She wanted to call Elizabeth and check that Cole was okay. How could she be away from her son at this time? She needed to get to him because she just wanted to hold him in her arms and feel that everything was going to be alright. In the face of it, everything seemed in tatters but there was no more Tommy which meant no more beatings, no more fear of her own shadow. Ellie could walk away from this and have the life she always wanted.

If only she could remember what she'd done.

Then, in her mind, she heard a different voice. She didn't recognise it at first. It spoke in hush tones, woke her from a slumber and made her feel like nothing was wrong. Like she would survive this just as she had survived everything else.

She rose from the solid surface and walked towards the cell door. How much longer had she to wait for someone to arrive from legal aid. She pressed against the door and faced the sandy coloured floor.

Even that made her depressed. Then, finally she remembered something that mattered.

Ellie slapped on the door until one of the uniformed officers arrived. She was standing face to face with the young man who had brought her tea earlier. The face of apparent evil meeting the perceived face of good. It was that primitive now.

'What can I do for you, Mrs. Hunter?'

Finally adding the next piece to the puzzle that had been grinding her for the past couple of days, she looked him dead in the eyes. 'I need to make a phone call. It's urgent.'

*

There wasn't much that couldn't be sourced from an internet search nowadays. As Simon sat outside the Calvay bar on the edge of the city centre, he noted that it looked like a remnant of a bygone area. Many of the doors alongside the bar looked vacant and as he nudged his head to the right, he found himself staring at a barren ground that looked caught in the midst of unfinished business.

Not that the place wasn't vibrant. He watched

Chris get out of his car and cross the street. He was discreetly parked at enough distance that he didn't think he would be noticed. He couldn't be sure Chris hadn't noticed him but if he did, he wasn't showing any sign of recognition.

The echo of a song blasted out from the bar and a couple of girls were in the doorway, dancing whilst surrounding themselves in a hue of smoke.

Chris was approaching and holding out his fist now. He bumped it into the fist of an older man who emerged from the bar. That was Sammy Winters, owner of the bar that he had inherited from his grandparents.

Simon stared down at his screen. He wondered what relationship existed between Simon and Sammy. He felt his stomach churn that anyone would ever break bread with Chris. Then, not everyone had a sister who died at the hands of Chris. Not everyone would appreciate the insidious underbelly of such a person.

Stepping out of the car just in time to see Chris enter the bar to an enthusiastic fanfare, Simon followed, now confident that he was anonymous enough to evade Chris. He positioned himself at a stool at the far end of the bar. He looked out the window and listened to a guitarist strum lightly in preparation for his evening gig. The loud club music that had been playing was now dead and the crowd had started to tune into the guitarist as he tried to find his key.

The atmosphere was buoyant, the crowd eclectic. Not at all what he might have expected from a bar in the deep East centre of Glasgow. The place may have existed in the derelicts of the city, but they'd managed to retain a certain ambience inside.

Yet, beneath the facade of jovial, Simon knew something wasn't right here. Suspicion gnawed. Something darker than he saw. Chris hadn't come here for a night of acoustic music. He had an agenda and Simon needed to know what it was.

The rain began outside. To avoid suspicion, he left before Chris returned to the bar. He dashed across the street and finally realised what it was that had been scratching at his nerves. He'd never lied to his family before. Not about anything. Just another notch on the growing list of deeds perpetrated by Chris. He suddenly felt guilty. Could he really blame the man for this? Maybe it was time to be a little more truthful, both with himself and with his family.

Simon settled back into his seat and started up the engine. A moment later, he made the decision that he'd been toying with for the past few days. He dialed the number of the one person he knew he could rely on.

CHAPTER TWENTY-SIX

It was a devastating loss. Richie had built those stables up one horse at a time and it was now one of the most prosperous horse shelters in the area. Now, all that was left was a black charred shell.

He could not tell Connie how he felt. Of course, he knew loss. So did she. Did he dare compare this loss to that of Lara? Of course, there was no comparison, but he knew all too well that even bringing it up would only open a brand-new can of worms and he usually ended up with them on his face.

Richie walked away from the burnt remains of his business and felt his heart sink because, though he still owned the horses, they were now scattered round several local places, and he suspected he was going to have a job proving that the fire had not been of his making. As soon as it was mentioned that the fire service suspected an accelerant, he knew he was in for a world of questions. He didn't have the answer to them.

He was disturbed then by the sound of his mobile phone ringing in his pocket. The song, despite being upbeat, left him feeling melancholy. It was one he enjoyed with Lara. In better times, it gave him a momentary smile. In times like these, hurtling towards the anniversary of her death and this latest tragedy, Richie buckled. He ignored the call, fell to the ground, and began to howl. Once more, life had played a cruel trick on him and his family and this time, Richie didn't feel he was strong enough to carry it all on his lagging broad shoulders.

*

Connie enjoyed when no-one was home. It made it all the easier to have a couple of vodka's without having to justify it by her awful day. Lying had become easy but she simply couldn't be bothered. This way, she could top herself up and feel absolutely justified in doing so. She listened to a collection of songs that Richie had made her on their last anniversary, their very own mixtape of their life together. She moved across the bedroom, pulling dresses from the wardrobe. It had been a long time since Connie had enjoyed playing dress up. It was a shame because she had some beautiful expensive clothes. Just a shame not to wear them.

She hit a brick wall though because at the end of the collection was the black Versace dress she had last worn to Lara's funeral. She occasionally came across it and knew it was just one more thing to remind her. Another thing that Bill Brady might encourage her to discard. She wouldn't discard it. The last time she had worn that beautiful frock, she had walked alongside her daughter's coffin and seen her off on her final journey. She placed it on the bed and looked at it, a mixture of fury and heartbreak but a pride that Lara would have seen her in it. Lara had often joined Connie in dress-up. Would she still enjoy it now? If there was one thing Connie prided herself in it was good taste. She was certain that Lara would have been the same.

Her mobile rang. She winced.

Picking it up, Connie answered and placed the handset to her ear. Then, she heard a confession she hoped never to hear.

*

Drew watched Stephanie settle their son, Oliver, and felt the urge to run. The last few days had been stressful, and he felt that his father had started to express doubt in his ability to run the stables. Truth was, Drew was doubting his own ability. How could this have happened? Even though he'd done nothing untoward in terms of the fire, he suspected the investigators would go further back. Would they see the historical mismanagement, the financial discrepancies or, indeed request to see Drew's own accounts?

He listened to his boy coo, and it warmed his heart a little. There wasn't a lot to be proud of at the moment, but Stephanie and Oliver countered that balance. He thought of Max, who hadn't been far from his mind in the past days and thanked God that Max had stepped in to help him escape the wrath of debt collectors. Max's help itself would eventually have come at a price. Drew knew that. He could only dine out on the fake-uncle connection so long. He suspected that when Max came to collect, he would pay dearly.

Was it wrong that he felt relief after learning of Max's death. After all, what they'd learned about Max's deviant behaviour made it a little easier to swallow what had happened to him. Deserved might be too strong a word, but karma did have its way.

He watched the mobile phone vibrate and begin to rotate round the smoked glass table. He leaned forward and knew the moment had finally arrived. As he answered the call, he suspected that the truth had finally been realised.

CHAPTER TWENTY-SEVEN

'Maggie, I need to speak to you in private.'

She dumped her newspaper on the staff room table and followed him out into the corridor.

Ryan smirked, a rare moment of cheer from a young man who had made a name for himself as Mr. Stern.

'What's made you so happy? Did someone kill a cat?'

'Now, now,' he implored, shocked that she thought this of him. 'I have two cats at home, and I'd be devastated if anyone hurt them.'

'Sorry,' she whispered, sheepishly as she leant against the corridor wall. 'So, what's happened?'

'So, you know we were wondering what happened to the charge that got lost in transit over at the airport?'

She narrowed her eyes and frowned. 'You mean the one that Max McDermott got Tommy off on?'

'Absolutely, except Max didn't get him off legitimately.'

She moved towards him, aware that traffic had busied up in the corridors. A slight ray of light rested on her face, splitting her face into two halves. 'Then, who did?'

Ryan looked round, careful to avert prying ears. He didn't feel ready to reveal the full details to those who might leak it to external sources. 'Guess who is currently paddling for his life over at headquarters and dropping an almighty bus on his friends and colleagues.'

'No,' she said, stretching the word out until her eyes had fully widened.

'Darren Philip worked with the border force at the airport for five years until he got caught with sticky hands. He was Max's right-hand man alright. Drugs, trafficking, illegal merchandise. You name it and he's spilling the beans on it right now. Tommy wasn't the only patsy who almost ended up with jail time, he was just lucky that it was his trial run and that it was small enough that Darren and Max could make it disappear.'

'It's unbelievable. I always wondered how

Philips could afford that house in Callander when he was on a layman's pay.'

'How the other half live,' said Ryan, his mood more flamboyant than it had been since arriving in this village. He had finally found a case complex enough to capture his interest and he truly dreaded the moment when it was over. He suspected this was a blue moon in Crianlarich and soon they'd be trying to find themselves the odd cold case to work on.

'Indeed. So, is Ellie off the hook for the murder then?'

'I don't know if she's innocent. We must ask her a few more questions before we send her home. I don't think Max or Darren had anything to do with it. Firstly, it is too passionate an attack. They probably don't care enough about Tommy to kill him. Besides, one is dead and the other probably didn't know the chickens were about to roost.'

'Let's get it over with then. I've called in someone I know who sometimes works legal aid.'

Darren might have told her to keep out of it and let the desk deal with that, but he knew how concerned Maggie was for Ellie. He decided not to make an issue out of it. He was learning that good officers sometimes allowed the lines to blur. Perhaps attracting bees with honey rather than vinegar might occasionally serve its purpose.

*

'Hi babe.'

Simon was back on the motorway now and he was staying far enough back to allow Chris the freedom to drive. 'Hey, Gor, how are you? I miss you.'

'Miss you too. Please come next time. I am so bored,' said Gordon, a light tapping penetrating the phone. 'What are you doing?'

'I've just come out for a drive. You know you're always telling me I should get out more.' He wondered if Gordon would hear the lie in his voice.

'Wow! Good for you. You do need to get out more. The house isn't good for you all the time.'

'Did you decide against going to the barbecue last night?'

'Yes, I'm seeing them on Sunday remember. I

think once a week with my family is more than enough. I hear that mum and Drew were having words about her drinking again. That's becoming a regular thing.'

'You agree with him?'

Simon pulled the car into the side of the road and paused. 'In some ways. I don't agree with the way he antagonises her, but I understand his concerns.'

'Then, don't get involved, babe. Your mum and Drew have wound each other up for as long as I've known them.'

'You're right,' said Simon, returning his focus to the car that was now disappearing round a winding road. They were forty minutes from the village by now. 'Listen, I'll go just now. I'm almost home.'

Another lie.

Gordon sighed. 'Honestly, really wish you were here.'

'Me too,' said Simon, genuinely wishing he was anywhere but here. He could still see the lights flood the dimming skylight as the Skoda rushed off ahead.

Simon felt his nerves heave, a sickness in his

stomach as he realised the enormity of what he was about to do. He put the car back into gear and pulled out into the road. Then, he hit the throttle and headed the engine into the hanging silver clouds.

CHAPTER TWENTY-EIGHT

Janie O'Reilly had inherited all Max McDermott's caseload. She didn't need it, nor did she want it but the poor unfortunates he'd abandoned needed her help. After all, not all of them were the hub of dead-end criminality. Some were the genuine needy. Much like this girl she was about to go and help.

The drive had been arduous. Some idiot in a Skoda had almost sped into the back of her, then flipped the bird when she had the audacity to stand up to him. She parked up and headed into the police station, checking that her pristine grey trouser suit remained untouched by the weary day and that her blouse had managed to escape the coffee spillages that always seemed to happen twenty minutes before she was due to be somewhere important.

She had listened to the police officer with grave interest. Janie suspected that most of Max McDermott's clients deserved a stint in jail. And he had represented the deceased in this case. Max couldn't have touched the young woman's defense even if he wanted to. Which he probably wouldn't have. So, Janie welcomed it. Max hadn't often led anyone to decency but having heard the suspected motivation for killing this Tommy Hunter, she rather appreciated that the young woman currently being held in the cells might just need a little helping hand.

'I'm here to speak with my client, Eleanor Hunter. Could you arrange for me to speak with her in a reasonably comfortable area.'

The young officer behind the counter looked startled, like he had just been visited by the mother of God herself. He stumbled outwards, nodding as he stared and fumbling with his pen.

'I'll have two sugar and one milk please. Whatever my client is having too. It's been a stifling day.'

'Yes,' he said, and made a run for the corridor.

It was harrowing to her that so little happened in these villages. Every time she was called to village stations, she was always astounded by how rundown they were, and usually manned by children. He may have been a similar age to her son but that didn't stop her making a beeline for his backside with her eyes.

A few minutes later, Janie sat across from the once pretty young woman now being interviewed by police for the murder of her husband. 'What have you said?'

'There's nothing for me to say,' snapped Ellie.

'Okay, good, stick with that for now. You need to remember that it is up to them to establish your guilt, not for you to prove your innocence.'

Ellie let her lank hair drop into the crevices of her hands. 'This is a nightmare. I've spent more time in a cell today than my husband ever did and he was actually guilty.'

She looked tortured, thought Janie, eyeing the girl's sunken eyes, emaciated body, and the way her lips looked poured onto her teeth. 'We will get to that, Eleanor.'

'Ellie,' snapped the girl.

'If there's anything in there that you're not sure of, you say no comment. If it feels like they're backing you into a corner, no comment. If they ask you your bra size, favourite song, or the time of your

GP appointment next Tuesday, you say no comment. Always no comment if you're less than sure of why they're asking.'

Ellie nodded.

'They will keep asking and eventually you will have to provide the answers. I don't want you to tell me if you're guilty. That, I don't care about but if I ask you anything and you lie to me....' Her eyes narrowed. 'I will leave you to rot. Do you understand?'

Ellie appeared to understand perfectly and after only forty minutes more in the interview room, she stood and walked out of that station with her head held high.

*

Simon's car thundered down the road so hard that it felt like it might fall apart beneath him. His foot trembled, a heat spreading up his leg as if he were about to pass through the atmosphere itself. He no longer cared what happened to himself because this route he had taken was no longer fully about him. Something in him had changed the moment he stood beneath the viaduct and watched the shadowy figure enter the abandoned Burns' house.

Now he had taken an oath. Not a religious vow, nor a promise to anything sacred. Rather, he had spoken of intent to inflict harm on someone who had destroyed something in him and his family long ago. Chris Burns had to die, and it had been his pledge to turn those wheels and make it happen. He didn't know how yet. The finer details hadn't been tapped into. However, he had to get to Chris now before he returned to the village. The words of wisdom had been spoken.

He felt the car bounce over a deep incline as he took each turn in the road. He could see the Skoda up ahead as he continued to press his foot to the pedal. He looked at the dial and saw he was now reaching eighty. He lowered the window and heard the wind rattle like thunder against the tip of the window. He inhaled breath, held it there just long enough for the cold to tickle and then took another deep turn.

Finally, he was nose to nose with Chris and he enjoyed just a little too much the look on Chris's face when he realised what was happening.

Simon leered as he drew up to the side of Chris and stared. He was on the wrong side of the road now but that was okay because he could see far enough ahead to shift aside should anything come towards him. Right now, he smiled because he had finally come face to face with the man who he blamed for ruining his family.

A slight nudge of the wheel to the left.

Simon's car slid alongside the steel work of the Skoda as Chris's eyes widened. Letting out a scream borne of both joy and rage, Simon turned the wheel once more, this time with more ferocity.

Sparks heralded the meeting of metal as Simon drew back and allowed the other car to shift forward. Then he slammed his vehicle into the bumper of Chris's car and watched joyously as the back of the Skoda rose from the tarmac.

Another scream.

He bumped once more, giving it a good proper thud. Then, he pulled back alongside the car and remembered the words that had been spoken.

'Get him off the road before he returns to this village. If anyone knows he's here, it'll be harder to make him disappear.'

With that burning in his mind, Simon's eyes settled on the other vehicle just in time to see Chris's hand rise up with a semi-automatic in his leather gloved grip.

CHAPTER TWENTY-NINE

Chris got the fright of his life. Not a little jolt when waking from an unwanted nightmare, but a nerve shredding shudder through his entire being as he saw the car move to the side of him. He'd noticed a while ago that the same car kept appearing in his rear-view mirror. Coincidence? He didn't believe so, but he didn't recognise the vehicle, nor the silhouette of the person behind the wheel.

He wasn't far from his house now. He would return and set the final wheels in motion to confront Richie and Connie. He needed them to understand, firstly that he had never harmed a hair on beautiful Lara's head. How strange that he needed them to know that before betraying her memory in such a fatal and destructive way. Secondly, he needed them to see him coming. No concealment. Not hiding behind the cyber world. For them, it was personal and with that in mind, revenge needed to be handed to them in person.

Of course, this was a new problem. Someone was

tailing him and as the car slammed into the side of him, Chris knew this had been no accident.

He tried to reach across to the passenger's seat so he could grab the gun but there was no time because the other car, a blue Honda, almost sent him careering off the road and into the woods. This couldn't be the end. There was too much to lose.

He thought of all he had done to mark his revenge, the destruction of all those lives and now the ultimate revenge that would make him feel it had all been worth it. Once again, he reminded himself he wasn't a bad man. He was a man who was taking back his own narrative after the ultimate betrayal.

He thought of his mother once more. Didn't she deserve to have a voice after all they'd taken from her. The Gibbs family had run the narrative for twenty years, everybody bowing at their grief-stricken victimised feet. Lara was simply a mascot for their propaganda, no longer a person in her own right but a face for an agenda that had robbed him and Cathy of their rightful relationship.

He tried to place those eyes. He felt like he

should recognise them. He looked to his right once more, steering hard enough to keep himself on the black snaking road, but the car was pulling back and now forcing him forward.

Chris leaned into the dashboard, slamming down on the accelerator, and navigating the gears. He checked his rear-view mirror once more, and he could see the black shape of the man reflecting back at him. The only way to fight now was to fight with bullets. He only had six loaded. He needed two of those if anything went wrong.

Finally, he was able to reach for the gun and tighten his hand round it. He lowered the window so that it gave him some exposure should the car come back towards him. He thought of all his regrets as the sun finally disappeared. An angry night sky descended upon them as Chris opened his window and felt the wind flush his skin.

The Honda sidled up to the Skoda once more and Chris finally recognised those eyes. They stared across, not the wide-eyed gaze of boyhood admiration anymore, but the dipped edge of sadness of a man in his thirties. Simon, Lara's youngest brother and someone who had eluded Chris's interest because he forgot to remember that even little boys grow up in the sundial of their mother's bitterness.

He raised the gun, a warning only because he had no desire to kill Lara's brothers. They were as innocent in all of this as he was, but he couldn't let the alternative happen.

They were reaching the bridge that separated Crianlarich from the busier nearby towns and Chris knew there was only room for one of them on there. His teeth chittered at the sound of the other car grinding into his, metal screaming as the vehicle was forced once more off to the side.

In that moment, Chris had no choice. He extended his arm out the window, pressed on the trigger, and saw the horrified look on Simon's face as he pulled back and fired a single bullet through the glass window of the empty seat in the next car.

*

Simon saw the recognition and then the confusion on his potential victim's face. He heard those words again. *Make him disappear.*

He had no choice now because he had reached out. Simon was no longer orchestrating this alone. He had handed the reigns over to someone whose motivations far surpassed his. He had learned of a hatred far stronger than his own, a desire for revenge that sprawled to landscapes he couldn't even imagine.

The other car was taking a hit. There was a gaping hole in the metal now and it made it all the easier to get it off the road. Of course, Simon hadn't prepared himself for the gun. Naturally that was what Chris must have collected form Glasgow. What other reason would he have for going there under the cloak of dusk?

Simon threw all his weight towards the wheel and moved about in his seat. He could not allow himself to be the target of Chris's bullet.

Wondering what his sister, now relegated to Sainthood status in his family, would think of all this, he tried to find a meeting point in his mind where Chris would not be the villain. There was no middle ground on that. Chris had given her those drugs. He'd taken her down to the lake. He'd laughed mightily as he watched her fall overboard and then struggle to get to the surface. Then he'd let her die on that pier because he was a weak will-less bastard who had thought of himself first.

There was no middle ground on this.

One more slam and then he saw the gun poke out the window and take aim. Simon knew he had to pull back if only just to let Chris pull that trigger and miss. It was hard though because the other car was now pulling back and staying in line with him.

Simon looked ahead. They were almost at the bridge, a small single file thoroughfare that would probably collapse under the weight of this conflict. It was, after all, simply made of bricks and rose only twelve feet above a tiny rockery that headed off at a nearby gorge.

Finally, the sparks flew as a bullet sprung from the gun.

Simon hat not a nano-second to waste. He slammed on the brakes, heard his tyres screech, and then slammed once more into Chris's side. The bullet had shattered the window, but the aim had been futile. There was not another chance to disarm the bastard. So, Simon let out one more roar and swung backwards, throwing his force down on the accelerator.

He watched in equal measure horror and pride as the other car met with the edge of the stone bridge and toppled sidewards down the quarry with an almighty clatter. Simon allowed his car to thunder over the bridge before slamming on the brake. He pushed so hard that it caused his vehicle to spin on two wheels and then screech to a sudden halt.

Looking around to ensure no-one else was around, Simon realised he had pressed his hand down on the passenger's seat where a rubble of broken glass now lay. He only knew it when he saw the blood trickle. It didn't matter now. There was no time for self-care or that kind of indulgence. He had to get back to the other car before Chris was able to escape.

CHAPTER THIRTY

Ryan rushed into the staff room where Maggie had settled for one last coffee of the day.

'What?'

'Is that any way to greet the man who is about to tell you who the killer is.'

She looked at him with feigned patience. Another sip from her coffee mug. 'We've spent all afternoon grilling a young woman who, by all accounts, is quite seriously traumatised. You're going to tell me that we have the evidence to arrest her, aren't you?'

Ryan dropped into the seat beside her. 'Why do you sound so cynical.'

She snarled. 'Because I AM cynical. We've just roasted a girl who should really be getting a Pride of Britain award for commuting a crime that I should be horrified by, but I'm too old and long in the molars to be remotely shocked by.' She paused for another sip from the mug. 'I know you're young and full of your own self-importance, but once you've been around this planet long enough, you'll find your way into a place where black and white no longer exists. You'll understand that good people have to do things to protect themselves from people like Tommy, and Max, and whoever else has wrecked this peaceful little place.'

'I've just had a call from the labs. They found some traces of a red fabric among the blood on Tommy's clothes. The first stabbing wound was fatal and delivered by the left hand. The other sixteen wounds were all delivered by the same instrument, most likely the missing knife from the block we retrieved from the lakeside. They were delivered slightly later and with the right hand. Possibly to throw us off the path and insinuate they may have been delivered by a different person.'

'What about the pendant you found? Did you identify those to whom it belonged?'

He moved closer to her, the lemon scent from his meringue reaching her nostrils. He pushed his phone across the table and pointed it the image of the pendant. 'I have indeed. Scroll out.'

She quickly began to scroll out and then she let

out a gasp. 'It can't be.'

He smiled. 'It is. Exact one. Forensics are dusting for fingerprints, but I wanted to ask you, Maggie, when you were at the crime scene the other day, did you notice anyone standing around?'

She shook her head, seemingly finding a new zest for this. Her weariness dissipated right before his eyes.

'Look here.' He tapped on the screen once more and this time, navigated to some of the crime scene photos. He was pushing through them, each one a map of Tommy's dead body. Then, some of other location photos came into view and Maggie found herself not looking at the dead body, but the bodies who stood around in horrifying awe of what had taken place here. 'Zoom in this time.'

She did as she was told and watched as the image became pixelated. It wasn't as clear now, but it was clear enough to show the red hooded jumper.

'We've been looking in the wrong place, Maggie. I would hazard a guess that our killer is the person standing right there. I'd put a month's pay on the fabric in Tommy's blood matching the fabric of that jersey.'

Maggie slammed the mug down. 'I'll take that bet and raise you on finding fingerprints that match on the pendant. How long are they going to take?'

'Not long but we'll have to apply for a warrant to make an arrest. The sooner we get this off our table, the sooner everybody can get on with their lives.'

She tusked and pushed his phone away. 'In some ways, I'm glad.'

Ryan gripped his phone and looked at her pale face. 'Why, glad?'

'Because I didn't believe it was Ellie in the first place. But did you see the look on her face? She wasn't sure. I think she would have held her hands up to it if we'd pushed hard enough. Aren't you glad we didn't?'

Ryan felt a little giddy inside. He'd cracked the case and managed not to throw a young widow under the bus though he still wasn't sure she wasn't involved in some way. 'I don't believe in sending innocent people to jail,' he muttered.

Maggie stood, grabbed the mug so she could return it to the kitchen and laughed knowingly. 'Yet, the prisons are littered with innocent people who nobody believes. That's why my cynicism is so vital. It leaves me less open to making the wrong judgement. Therefore, people like Ellie can get a fair hearing.'

He watched her shuffle away before she paused and turned to him.

'Well, are you coming?'

He narrowed his eyes. 'Coming where?'

She placed her hat atop her head and adjusted it. 'To arrest Little Red Riding Hood of course.'

*

The collision reverberated throughout the silent night. Even the wind appeared to halt as a single lone owl rested on a nearby branch and hooted.

Simon stared down. The blood muddied the black waters of the stream but only momentarily before fading into the depths and disappearing completely. There was enough light that Simon could see exactly what he'd done, though he reminded himself this was an instruction that would allow him to deliver vengeance whilst also returning to his unscarred life.

The toppled car threatened to fire up, the sparks clicking as Simon stood over it and hoped that it wouldn't explode. He didn't care about Chris, but he cared enough about himself that he didn't want to die in a fiery ball. He closed his eyes and heard a groan. Was Chris calling out to him for help?

It was help that would never come because Simon had gone too far. He'd only gone as far as this because of what Chris had put his family through. So many lives destroyed after the death of Lara and subsequently in the past few days because of what Chris had done.

Finally, he settled on what had to be done. Simon reached for a rock and wondered, not for the first time since looking down what it might feel like to crush that skull. Was there a more deserving victim? He would soon know.

Simon rested his free hand on the edge of the toppled car and moved closer. Once he was only an inch from Chris's face, he whispered through broken tears, 'This one's for my sister.'

Then he brought down the rock and waited for life to drain from Chris's terrified eyes.

*

Nobody else would understand quite like her. As she gently brushed his face, he looked at her with such pride. How did a thirteen-year-old get so lucky?

'Lara, you should become a make-up artist when you grow up?'

She hooted with laughter, that same infectious laughter he'd heard all his life. Except when she was slamming the door and screaming the house down, but it had bene a while since she'd thrown one of her infamous strops. After all, nobody could out-strop the real diva of the house. Connie had that market coveted before Lara could even speak.

'And you should become a drag queen. You have the perfect bones for it.'

Simon felt giddy. Like they had just entered their own secret little world that no-one would invade. 'I want to be a painter, but I want to be beautiful like you.'

'My dear,' she said, emulating a voice that might have sat well with the hoi-polloi. 'You are beautiful like me. In fact, in some countries and cultures you might be more beautiful. Look at that bone structure. Tres magnifique.'

Simon chuckled, wondering what his father might say if he walked in. Richie had tried to steer his boys into the same manly profession he himself had ventured into, but he'd misjudged Simon, who much preferred the company of the women in his family.

Lara brought round the mirror and tenderly stroked his face. 'You see how beautiful you are, Si. Inside and out.'

Simon didn't see. He only saw a boy with make-up on and it made him want to cry. He thanked whatever God had created him that he'd been given this wonderful complimentary sister because he knew Drew had little interest in him and that this particular moment might be the source of many uncomfortable moments in the future.

'I want to wash it off now,' said Simon, tears

forming.

Lara pulled him to her in a tight hug. 'Certainly, you can but not because someone else tells you to. Okay? You are amazing, Si. The best little brother a girl can practice her contouring on. You don't need to cry, sweetheart. Just because you don't like the things dad and Drew like, doesn't mean they're any better than you.'

Simon sniffed, forced back some of the tears and then hugged her back. He was sure that to some people Lara might just be a little girl but to him, she was the almighty goddess that bred life beyond Crianlarich. It was the life he might find one day and only because her words had encouraged it.

'Right, anyway, let's get you cleaned up before dad gets home.' She began to softly wipe his face and as he looked in the mirror, he could see how much alike they were. He loved his brother Drew, but he didn't like him all the time. With Lara, there was no middle ground, no dubiety. He watched in admiration as she deftly restored him to the sullen little boy that the rest of the world recognised. Inside, though, he

had found his inner fabulous and he never wanted to lose that again.

CHAPTER THIRTY-ONE

Connie

The second glass of Chardonnay took the edge off. Just enough to decide that she would wear the dress. It felt right, like the momentous occasion upon her required it.

Connie peeled off the red hooded top, catching sight of the logo as she discarded it onto the floor. She hadn't dared ask Richie if the company was in trouble because she wasn't sure she would like the answer. There were times she felt the running of that business was none of hers and since opening the florists, she was even less inclined to offer an opinion. Besides, Richie had always been such an astute man, she couldn't imagine he would have let things slip. Drew was a different story.

She was still fusing. The phone call had thrown her for a curve and now she was struggling to steady her nerves as she held the long-stemmed glass in her small hand.

Pulling the dress on, she amazed herself because it still fitted and if she squinted just enough, she might have been transported back two decades. Despite everything, Connie had cared for herself. She'd had the odd secret procedure that not even Richie had commented on, taken care of her skin, and had worked out just enough that her body had stayed in shape. Her one vice was alcohol, but she didn't even drink that much. Despite what her controlling older son might claim.

She ran her fingers down the soft fabric and closed her eyes. How was it possible that one piece of fabric could take her back to a time she had once been in loathe of but now harked back to so often. There was something about the days after Lara's death where it felt so fresh and where she didn't have to apologise for being in the thick of her grief. The reaction to her pain hadn't been gratuitous. It had simply been accepted. Now she felt like mentioning Lara's name was hyperbolic. There was a tiny hidden space hidden away that she reserved for those who appeared to begrudge her that grief the most.

She looked at the clock on her bedside cabinet and saw it was just after nine PM.

Descending the stairs, Connie caught her slimline figure in a mirror on the top deck of the stairs and envied her own curves because she knew beneath the fabric, it didn't really look like that.

She held her mobile phone in her hand, clinging to it like it was her lifeline. She was waiting on news. News that wasn't coming fast enough. She entered the kitchen, soft footed so as not to disturb Richie if he was home. She didn't want him to know she was going out. She didn't need the questions. They had enough on their plate, he would say. He was right, but being right didn't matter right now.

Connie pulled a vodka bottle out that was almost empty, and she poured it across clinking ice inside a glass. In her head, now spiraling it sounded like clashing icebergs echoing in a crashing storm. It jaded her. Her eyes nipped, the lower sacks weighing heavily with the burdens from the last few days. She needed to get this over with.

So, still determined not to disturb Richie if he

was home, Connie entered her car and searched the lower dash for some mint gum. Then, against every fiber of her judgement, she turned on the ignition and waited for the phone to ring. Now, all she was waiting on was the nudge and then she would be on her way to finish what had started all those years ago.

CHAPTER THIRTY-TWO

The drive round the curves of Crianlarich might have been more enjoyable if not for the sirens and the blue lights. The DNA results on the red hooded top had come back in the last few minutes, as had some of the DNA on the pendant. They had pinpointed the perpetrator and they were heading to the heights of those hills to make an arrest.

Maggie looked pleased that Ellie would be in the clear, but she still had her reservations. 'The Gibbs family have been through enough. I wish we had a way of drawing a line under this.'

'That's not the way the law works,' Ryan reminded her.

'I didn't say it was. It doesn't mean I can't dream.'

He didn't speak then because he had realised that Maggie was guided as much by her own heart as she was by her police instincts. It didn't make her any less productive as an officer. In fact, he had come to admire her love of this village and the way she was able to combine duty and care without compromising herself.

'I hope we've got this right,' he said, voicing a rare moment of doubt.

'So do I,' she said, turning the wheel as they continued to rise up the hills until they were eyeline with the steeple of the chapel.

'DNA is rarely wrong nowadays. You know that, don't you?'

Maggie bit down on her lip. 'I know it and most of the time, I appreciate it. Not today. I am about to arrest someone for killing a person who made a pretty pitiful human being.'

'That's not for us to judge, though. A court of law may well take into consideration what Ellie has gone through with Tommy. Or perhaps they'll remind his killer, and anyone deemed to do the same thing that the police are there for a reason.'

Maggie lowered the window slightly and took in a little of the mid-evening air. 'Sorry, it's an age thing.'

Suddenly, Ryan was back in that awkward arena

where he wished he hadn't exposed any of his self-doubt to her. Maggie didn't need much encouragement to speak candidly so he wouldn't give her an additional opportunity.

'Not long to go now,' she said.

Ryan sat in the passenger's seat and felt a trickle of excitement. The donkey work had been done. Now all he had to do was make the arrest. He may well have agreed with Maggie that Ellie didn't deserve to have this ruin what little semblance of a life she still had. The killer did not deserve the same. This had been malicious and unnecessary. The one thing Ryan felt he might have gotten if he had held on long enough was motive. He was certain Ellie might have had insight even if she didn't know it. That ship had sailed when the white-haired granny had swept through the interview room and pulled rank. From what little he knew of the Gibbs family though; they would lock horns and it was going to take a vice to get that information out of them.

*

Simon had blood on his hands. He believed he'd done

what any decent son and brother should do. He'd defended the honour of his family. It had been hard but in the end, he didn't feel remorse. Why should he? Had Chris showed any remorse for Lara? Would he show any for the Gibbs family who he planned to dislodge a bullet into.

His destination lay ahead. All he had to do was get there and this would finally be over.

Unlike the rest of his family, Simon felt deeply. He hadn't been able to move forward like his brother or his father. He mirrored his mother in more ways than he sometimes admitted but he knew even she worried because Simon kept so much to himself. He was just the ticking time bomb that neither his family nor Gordon needed.

He stared into his own eyes, the burning mystery of himself that even he didn't fully understand. After all, had he ever considered that he was capable of murder? He'd been driven to tension many times at the thought of Chris Burns, but he'd never imagined fully realising murder. Now, he'd gone to a darkness in himself he didn't even know existed. He'd done it for the people he loved. That would always be his justification.

'You'll never get away with this.'

Simon turned and saw that Chris was awake.

His blood-soaked face was charged with rage. He wrestled against the knots of his bound wrists.

If Simon knew nothing else, he knew that the silence would burden Chris, so he said nothing. Though, he did slam on the brake just enough to cause Chris to lurch forward and almost fall from the leather seat.

Chris cried out.

Simon grunted in laughter. Then, he slammed on the accelerator and made the last dart towards the silver lake.

*

Connie had reached the car in one piece. She had also made it inside without dropping the key. The night air had hit her, and she suddenly realised she had probably drunk more than she had first thought. It bewildered her when she thought of the amount of times she had near misses and yet still no one realised that she was half plastered to the wall.

Of course, Connie suspected that most people knew but dared not say.

She got behind the wheel and looked out across the village, the view from their ridge side house proving to be quite the spectacle.

Tonight, the spectacle came with a deep shade of blue as the local constabulary hit the streets of this ordinarily sleepy village. Plenty had happened over the past few days to warrant such a presence though Connie was certain she could hear sirens rise up and edge closer.

She worried for her boys. The stable fire had really made her question what was going on with Drew and she suspected Richie might be the same. She had never needed to be a mother lion for that boy but that didn't mean she wouldn't be. One day he would need her and when that time came, Connie's claws were sharpened.

She might not say it often, but she could not bear to think of anything happening to him or Simon. Not now, not ever.

She opened the window once the car started up and she questioned the wisdom of driving into the mouth of the dragon. If the police were out tonight, it meant something was unfolding here and she didn't really want to be part of it. It was too late though. The phone call had started something that even she couldn't draw away from.

She shook her leg violently, nerves tingling, and she thought for a moment she might vomit. Looking down, Connie saw that the gut of the dress had begun to fold into itself. Perhaps she wasn't as trim as the mirror had suggested. The deceitful eye of vodka and wine.

She shifted the car into gear and heard it judder. Then, she let it go to the biting point just a little too quick and the engine died.

Still, Connie was determined not to give up. She would get there even if she had to walk in her kitten heels. Nothing was going to stop her ending this. Not even a temperamental car under the direction of a secret drunk.

CHAPTER THIRTY-THREE

Drew arrived. He had waited for this moment ever since he found out the truth. He could taste the Chilies on his lips, though it wasn't the burning sensation that caused him to smart. It was the audacity.

He stared sidewards at the sparkling lake, the real caravan of all the evil that had happened to his family. Sure, he had learned some harsh truths that belied everything he'd previously believed. How naive he had been, but it was those serpentine waters that had really taken everything.

Not that it mattered. Mere mortals couldn't beat nature. So, the blame had to go somewhere, and Drew could finally face where that blame lay.

His heart hurt. For twenty years he'd tried to be man enough to live outside the parameters of his mother's grief, tried to walk in the fine lines of his father's truth and had often scoffed at his emotional younger brother who wanted so badly to hang on to someone he barely knew.

He took a step forward, the heartache threatening to paralyse him. He continued to walk, seeing the silhouette in the midst of turmoil. Once he neared the scene, he looked from side to side. He'd already had one lucky escape and he wasn't sure he would be so lucky this time round.

Whatever happened tonight, he could not go to jail for murder. No matter what transpired, Drew had to make sure he stayed on the right side of the prison walls. He loved Stephanie and Oliver too much to miss out on years of their lives. He just hoped that his family would have his back on this.

*

It was easy to slip into an alternative narrative, realised Connie. She had been able to see the past in shaded dimensions. Even her sometimes-fraught relationship with Lara had become coloured by grief. She pulled the car over and calmed herself by speaking matter-of-fairly into the free air.

Connie fiddled with the radio. She needed something to keep her alert. It frightened her to turn those corners and feel the lids of her eyes dip so urgently. The last thing her family needed was for her to be found dead at the bottom of a cliff side. She took a moment to collect herself and then she put the car back into gear.

The song on the radio was an old one by Atomic Kitten. A song from around the time Lara died.

Connie began to sing along. In her mind, the vibrant young woman who had become an enigma to her was floating round the kitchen, so ethereal she might have been a ghost before she had even left the earth.

Connie could almost smell the perfume from the girl's skin.

She could hear the soft lull of a teenage sing-a-long that had started out vibrant and strong but then become the faded memory of a voice lost in the wind.

Connie sped up. She needed to get to the village. This had to end and end before the police got to her. She cursed under her breath. Then, she turned one more corner and sped past an army of police cars. She slowed up, hoping that no-one recognised it, that no-one was looking for her and most importantly that nobody detected she was more than just a little intoxicated.

She wondered if Richie had known she was gone yet. He would not approve of her decision at all. But she'd been given no choice. Tonight, all three of her children needed her and she would never let her beautiful daughter down again.

CHAPTER THIRTY-FOUR

Ellie moved round the house, packing up the things that she felt she might need. She also wanted to discard all of Tommy's things before she left the village. It was imperative that this was over tonight. She needed to confront the truth. She now knew there was little chance she had killed her husband. So, if she didn't strike the killing blow, then who did? She suspected she had gotten it right, but she wouldn't know until she looked into those eyes.

She had contacted a killer. Asked them to come here. Someone she had trusted in the past but now suspected their own preservation was more important than protecting her.

Time trickled off to a sullen swirl, dragging on with little regard for those who were caught in it. The air was moist now, the rain washing off the last remnants of summer.

Finally, she looked out the window and saw him standing there. He used to be someone she trusted. Now, she didn't even trust herself. She took a deep breath and prepared herself. In moments to come she would hear things that would destroy her love for a family who had almost been here own. Had they all been in it together, she asked herself? She no longer believed in the goodness in people.

It was time to go. She just had to hear this truth before she closed the door for once and for all.

*

Connie didn't want to move. The final showdown was set. She looked down onto the pier and began her panoramic glance across the horizon. She had arrived at the place where her heart had shattered twenty years ago – the very spot where she had last seen Lara. The myriad of anger, hurt, pain, grief, and resentment washed over her, threatening to overwhelm her already slightly inebriated mind.

She had expected to see her nemesis, Chris Burns, waiting on the pier, but as she approached, she saw her husband Richie instead. His posture was hunched, his shoulders weighed down by sorrow. Connie's heart ached at the sight of his distress.

'Richie,' Connie whispered, her voice trembling

with emotion. 'Why are you here?'

'He's coming here, you know. Chris fucking Burns.' His voice was infused with a bitterness she didn't recognise.

Richie turned, and his eyes met hers, red and swollen from crying. 'Connie, I didn't want you to come here alone,' he said, his voice breaking. 'I can't believe he's here. Whatever you've asked Si to do, I don't want him paying the price for this.'

Connie put her hand in his and tightened her teary eyes. She looked out into the very spot where she last saw Lara's lifeless body. 'I want him dead,' she muttered through gritted teeth.

She leaned in and embraced him, finally realising that his grief, whilst nurtured differently was no different from hers and that the gaping big hole she had existed in didn't belong solely to her. The weight of her grief was suddenly shared, and she felt the walls of anger and resentment start to crumble. 'I'm so sorry, Richie,' she whispered. 'I didn't always see your pain either.'

They stood there, holding each other, their tears

mingling with the saltwater breeze. In that moment, they were united.

Connie pulled away slightly, her eyes locking with Richie's. 'I know we need to move on, but not until we get closure,' she said with unfaltering determination. 'I don't want him breathing the same air as my grandson. I want him to pay for what he did. Disappearing for twenty years isn't good enough. He needs to be gone for good.'

Richie nodded. 'I think he burnt down my stables. I also think its him that unearthed all that filth about Max and Darren.'

'There's probably lots more we don't know. He came here for revenge. He thinks the state of his sorry miserable life is because of us.' Connie took a deep breath, feeling her resolve. 'Okay,' she said, her voice steady. 'We do this on our terms. Tonight, we get justice for our daughter and for our family and we can finally move on.'

Richie nodded in agreement. 'Agreed.'

As they stood on the pier, they waited with trepidation. Connie had given the order and she believed her son, however sweet he had always been, had the brass to take that order and carry it out. She knew he would do anything for her and now, in turn, she would do anything to protect him. Should Chris Burns ever be found, wherever his body ended up, she would always protect Simon. She would do his sentence, stand in front of him, take a bullet for him even. The one thing she would never allow was for his life to be ruined by this. Chris Burns would be the one to pay the price. She wouldn't allow any of this to touch her sons.

CHAPTER THIRTY-FIVE

The baby was awake. How could he not be when the police had almost taken the door off the hinges?

Stephanie rubbed her eyes and moved to the door, irritated that Oliver had only just settled.

'Okay, I'm coming,' she shouted, her voice sleepy after a day on the phones. She did not like evening visitors without them at least phoning ahead. It gave her the jitters, especially when Drew had gone out.

'Mrs. Gibbs,' said the man in the grey suit. He held up his warrant card. 'I'm looking to speak to your husband, Andrew Gibbs.'

'He's not here,' she said, wondering why the hell the police would be here at this late hour. She turned to look at Maggie, scowling in anger at the disruption. 'What is this about?'

Maggie squinted and adjusted her hat. 'We need to ask him some questions, love. Do you know when he'll be home?'

'Not a clue,' answered Stephanie, sharply.

'Maybe you'll consider coming back when my son isn't sleeping.'

Maggie looked at her apologetically, but she would get no such response from Detective Starling.

Curiosity eventually got the better of her. 'Is this about the fire?'

Ryan frowned, a crease forming on his otherwise taut skin. 'Not at all. I believe the fire at the Red Riding stables is in the hands of the appropriate authorities. Why? Do you have something you need to tell us?'

'No,' she said, shrilly. 'I only asked a bloody question.' She was still fraught from the idea that she would take another hour to get Oliver back to sleep. She winked at Maggie but didn't give Ryan the benefit of her humour. 'As I said my husband isn't here. I don't know when he'll be back, but I doubt he'll be able to help much with whatever it is you're investigating tonight.'

Ryan was about to put his hand on the door.

Stephanie slammed it. 'Pompous arsehole,' she said, neither up nor down if he heard her or not.

She heard the muffled conversation between Ryan and Maggie but couldn't make out the entire content. She heard Tommy Hunter's name mentioned though. It was enough to send a chill down her spine.

*

The decision was made, and Connie, once again, took the lead. This time, the stakes were higher, and she was willing to get her hands dirty, driven by an unyielding determination. She just hoped Simon hadn't failed, perhaps overthrown by Chris.

In the midst of their discussion, Richie suddenly opened up, seizing the opportunity to express his thoughts.

'I think often of Cathy Burns,' he admitted softly.

'I don't see the point in squandering a thought on someone who doesn't deserve it. Or your pity, Richie. If she hadn't brought that nightmare into the world, my daughter would still be alive today.'

Richie always knew when he was defeated. It was written across his face. However, this one time, he wasn't giving up. 'You know the boys used to still do odd jobs for her or deliver her shopping. She was as much a victim as anyone else.'

'Sorry,' she screeched, baring her teeth. 'Are you mad? Have you got PTSD because your bloody stables burned down? That woman did not deserve your pity. If she had raised him right in the first place, perhaps he wouldn't have drugged my girl and then left her to drown.'

He blushed, a sure sign that he knew when to stop.

Connie wrestled with herself because she knew that she needed a drink now more than ever, but she wouldn't succumb. She wasn't moving until she knew Chris was dead. 'I tried to raise the boys to be kind,' she finally admitted. 'Drew was always yours. Simon was mine and, heaven help me, I adore him but maybe I was just a little too soft.'

'Don't say that,' ordered Richie, a man's man but no less proud of his youngest son. 'I wouldn't change him for the world.'

Connie's thoughts shifted. 'Did you know that monster was back in town? Has he just been swanning around like he owns the place? I swear if he's gone near that cemetery, I will make this as painful as it can be.' She stopped then, feeling her eyes widen in disbelief. 'You don't think its him that killed Tommy, do you?'

'No, I did not. I would have marched him out of town myself had I known. But I doubt he'll confess to any of it.'

She hadn't thought of that, but it made perfect sense. She realised that it was all very coincidental that there had been the two deaths, then the arrest of Darren Philips and the destruction at the stable. None of it had been murder directly, though? Was he capable of such an act? Perhaps him and Tommy could meet up in hell, exactly where both of them belonged.

At that very moment, in the momentary silence, Simon's car approached, flooding the area with light. Connie was visibly relieved that Simon had returned safely.

When Simon got out of the car, Connie was shocked to see him covered in blood.

'What the hell has happened to you?' She was shrieking as she picked up speed and ran towards him.

Simon stepped forward calmly and cocked his head to the back seat of the car. 'It's not my blood.'

Connie peered inside and made the chilling discovery – Chris Burns, almost unrecognizable, bloodied and bound in the back seat.

Despite the pitiful sight before her, Connie couldn't muster any sympathy for Chris Burns. The years of torment and anguish had hardened her to any pity she might have felt, leaving no room for mercy. Nothing would change her mind now. She wouldn't question the morality of it because as far as she was concerned, the hands of fate had cast its spell on them years ago.

Connie's only fear was that she would lose sight of herself now. She had never been a violent woman but there were things that would drive even the most placid soul to kill. In the end, the only thing she could do was see through what Simon had started.

'Simon, love. I want you and your dad to get him

to the boat. Throw him in and then I want you to leave.'

'What?'

She grabbed his face and caressed it softly. 'I want you to do what I tell you. You've done enough. This was never your fight. It's mine. He came back here for me. I know it. I'm the last person in his sick twisted game. So, let him have me and we'll see who comes out of it standing.' She spat on the ground, a momentary lapse in dignity.

'I can't leave you mum. Dad won't let you do it.'

'Your dad is going with you,' she said, catching Richie's furious eye. 'I can handle this. I want to handle this. I owe it to my Lara.'

Richie didn't argue with Connie because he must have known how determined she was. He simply opened the back door to the car and took the hit when Chris threw his legs out and began to kick wildly. Richie grabbed a piece of rope that had been discarded on the car floor and held it up. 'Don't make this more unpleasant than it has to be.

Chris snickered. 'Do you think I'm going to

make this easy for you, Gibbs?'

Richie wrapped the rope round Chris's ankles, just as if he were knotting up a hog. Then, he leaned in and pulled under the gap in Chris's arm. 'Get out.'

Connie shuddered and closed her eyes because even behind the mask of blood, she couldn't bear to look at him. She would only be happy to meet him eye to eye when he was taking his last breath. Right now, she had no desire to see him.

Simon grabbed his other arm and helped his father drag Chris towards the boat.

Finally, Connie would get the retribution she had always wanted. Eyes still tightly closed, she envisioned Lara's face, caught in the clouds as if she was nothing more than a wisp in the sky.

She finally opened her eyes just in time to catch Richie launching Chris's body into their old speedboat.

CHAPTER THIRTY-SIX

He was wearing the red hooded sweater with his company logo on it. It was the brightness of it that cemented in her mind what had happened. He'd been wearing it the other night.

'Why?'

Drew walked through the hallway, his muddy feet crunching on her wooden floors. 'Maybe for the same reason you thought you'd killed him. He had it coming.'

'Nobody has that coming,' she finally said, drawing breath and feeling determined that she would finally stand up for what was right. 'Why is it that men think they have the right to exert control over everyone with violence?'

Drew slid onto a chair and stared across the room, fixing his eyes on the radiator. The knife lay atop. 'So, you found it then. When did you know it was me?'

'Truthfully,' she said, pausing momentarily as she ran her mind over everything that happened.

'When I opened the door to you just then. I honestly didn't know what to believe. In fact, for some of the past few days I was questioning whether I had done it and just forgotten. I need to know why, though.'

Drew placed his head on his hands. 'I'm not going to jail for this.'

She shook her head slightly, looked at the units where the photos of her children used to sit. 'Did it happen here?'

He looked up.

'It happened here where my children slept,' she said, her voice infused with bitterness.

His face tightened, not the face of remorse but rather an accusing tone that suggested there was more to the story than he'd revealed.

'Did you know that he called me on the night he died?'

Ellie rounded the coffee table, sat on the edge with her hands under her. 'Why did he call you?'

'He had things to tell me. Things he wanted me to know.'

She froze.

'Do you know what those things were, Ellie? Did he admit to you what he was going to tell me?'

It felt like her blood turned to ice and had stopped pulsing through her. She wasn't sure she wanted to know what he would say next. Perhaps she already knew.

'Shall I let him tell you himself?'

Ellie stood. Was this some kind of sick game? 'Tommy's dead. He can't tell me anything.'

Drew stood and reached for her arm, pulling her closer. 'You know that when a person is murdered, the police say there is no better storyteller than the dead person themselves. They are the best witness to their own death. Their entire story is locked up there within them and it just takes the right investigator to unlock it.'

Ellie pulled away from him, just in time for him to grab her and dig his hand into her shoulder.

'Well, what if the person tells their story before they've even died? What if it's all here forever immortalised?' He held up his spare hand and in it was his mobile phone.

'I don't know what you're talking about.' Her voice quivered, terrified of what he was going to show her.

'Let's hear from the man of the moment, shall we.' He tapped on the screen and hit the play button.

Ellie's heart almost stopped in the instant that she heard her husband's raspy voice.

*

Connie stared in disbelief. If she didn't know better she would have expected to wake up any minute now. It was like that endless nightmare she had endured, the one with the scream that had begun the very night her daughter had been found dead and had lasted all the way through the infinite years. She could hear it now, in fact. All part of the same mobius loop that just went round and round, an endless trip in her mind that forever cemented her to that moment.

Of course, none of it was a dream. It only manifested itself in that way during the empty moments in between. This wasn't an empty moment. This was the other side of Lara's story, the one where she got to exist outwith the myth that her life had become. That's all Connie wanted now, to remove her daughter from that ghoulish hall of horrors retained for those who didn't make it all the way to the end of their rightful timeline.

Chris spat blood out and coughed. He looked in pain, though his expression wasn't complete behind the veil of facial hair and drying blood.

'You look fifty years old,' she finally said. It was the first time she had said anything remotely human to him and as she said it, it made her wish she could strip the layer of her tongue that allowed those words to pass.

'Thanks,' was all he could muster.

'You've been busy, haven't you,' she said, not knowing why she was entering into a conversation with him. After all, she had ordered her son to bring him here with the determination that he would die tonight. She was curious though because she wanted to know why he'd engaged in this game of cat and mouse with the people of Crianlarich. 'How long have you been planning this?'

He shook his shoulders in an attempt to loosen

the knots behind his back.

She snickered, looked up and waved Simon and Richie away. Then, she took a step down into the boat, and kicked Chris's legs to the side. 'I don't believe you ever intended to harm Lara,' she finally said. 'It was never about the intention though. It was about the final outcome. You can't undo what happened to Lara or what you did to the rest of us in the process. You wrecked our lives.'

'I didn't wreck anyone's life,' he replied, then coughed once more. 'Why won't anyone believe I wasn't even fucking there.'

Connie turned to see that Richie and Simon continued to watch. Why weren't they leaving, she wondered? She wanted so badly to save them from this. Richie was a good man. He could never knowingly hurt someone, and Simon had only acted in a way that he thought she wanted him to. She hadn't. Richie was right. She had raised Simon in her own image, without the bitter side that could not let go of this terrible thing that had devoured her entire life. In the end, though, they couldn't leave her anymore than she could leave them.

'Connie, I swear it to you. I was not there. I did not give Lara drugs. I didn't leave her to die. Why would I leave her to die and then go back when it was too late?'

She looked away in disgust. 'I don't know why people like you do the things you do. All I know is my beautiful little girl was drugged and left to drown.' She reached down, fury engulfing her so that it actually fed from her words. She grabbed his facial hair and pulled hard. 'I don't need a confession from you. I already know what you did. Keep lying if it makes you feel better but innocent men don't come back to the hallowed ground of their crimes and destroy more lives.'

He laughed then, the possible pre-cursor to his own death. 'You're talking about Max McDermott. He was filth. He raped a child and then added the insult of paying her for it. His friend Darren was no better. He shielded him for years. He also blackmailed him in secret so the two of them were as complicit as each other.'

'I don't care what they did. You're a murderer.'

'I haven't killed anyone, Connie. That's the hilarious thing,' he said, taunting her. 'After tonight, you might be a killer, and I'll still be fucking innocent.'

She reached down once more, ran her fingers through his blood. 'You see this, this is the least of what you deserve. I'm only sorry your mother isn't here to see it. That would really have been the daily double for me.'

He wrestled in anger then, kicked his feet against the edge of the boat. He pulled his head back and began to wrangle furiously.

Connie looked upwards at her son. Then, she noticed that something poked out of his pocket. She had contemplated how she would do this. It seemed poetic to force him into the water and watch him drown just as Lara had. She realised now it would be an insult to her daughter's memory to even suggest he grace the same waters she died in.

'Give me that.'

Simon turned to look at his father as if he were

waiting on the soft voice of reason.

'Give it to me,' she screamed, snapping her fingers viciously. She watched with cold dead eyes as Simon pulled the gun from his pocket. She felt it in her hand, like an extension of herself as he handed it down to her. Then, she turned it on Chris and allowed the adrenalin to race to her head. 'One of these is all it's going to take.'

CHAPTER THIRTY-SEVEN

'Drew, mate. It's Tommy. No hassle. You're obviously busy. I'm just phoning because Ellie kicked me out again. A-fucking-gain. Things haven't been good for years. I don't even think Cole is mine. I'm sure she was sleeping with somebody. Fuck's sake, mate, it could have been you. Your lot always defend her. Lie for her, even. You wouldn't be so quick to defend her if you knew what she was really like. That little bitch. She took us all in, mate. She's been lying to your face for years. You think her tears are because Lara died. Her tears are because she's terrified you find out the truth about what she did. What we did in fact. Listen, mate. Call me back. I'll tell you everything. That little bitch wants you to think she's an angel. If it wasn't for her, your sis would still be alive. Call me back, mate.'

*

Chris had managed to free the knot round his wrists and was now waiting patiently for his next move. He was past trying to explain what had happened on the night of Lara's death. That ship had long since sailed and sank.

'Just go,' said Connie.

Chris would take advantage of the pause because he suspected that she didn't want to pull that trigger in front of her son. After all, there were many things people could forgive but few could un-see their mother committing murder. Even Connie had a line she wouldn't cross.

Chris was free. He had finally managed to untangle the length of rope and all he had to do now was free his ankles. That would come but right now he just had to strike at the right moment.

Connie hissed then. She was buying time perhaps. 'What was your ultimate goal here? Huh? Come and destroy the people who loved Lara.'

'No,' he replied. 'I loved Lara. You never understood that. I came here to destroy the people who destroyed me, my mother and Lara's memory for me.'

'And you failed,' she said, gleefully.

'Not entirely. I brought this fucking village to its

knees. I may not finish you off Connie, but my intention was never to kill you. Or anyone, for that matter. The fact that Max killed himself was a pleasing little bonus but not the ultimate goal.'

'So, what was your plan towards us then. Burn down our business and that would equal what you feel you've lost.' She leaned down so close that he could smell the alcohol on her breath. 'That you think a horse stable anywhere equals my daughter's life shows what little you thought of her.'

He recoiled at her anger, at the bitterness of her words and realised that perhaps he hadn't quite gone far enough after all.

She grabbed him. 'Every morning I wake up, I wish I didn't. Then, I hear her voice in my head, and I figure I might just get through the day. I creep up to the cemetery because the thought of not being close to her makes me want to tear out my own heart and stomp on it. When I go for dinner with my family, I pray there's an extra seat there just so I can close my eyes and hear her speak to me. For as long as I can pretend, I can live. Do you honestly think your meagre pitiful little crush on her comes close to matching that.'

Chris looked at her through bleary eyes. How he wished he could move faster because his entire body ached. His shoulders felt like they'd been gripped down by a truck. His head was in agony, and he could feel the spot where he'd been hit earlier. Shards of glass pierced his arm, and he feared that pulling them out might injure an arterial spot that would cause him to bleed out. Still, he had to defend himself.

Connie cocked the gun and looked up at Simon. 'Ironically I believe he probably intended this for us. At least in the end you'll have died by your own hand. Just like your sad, pathetic little mother.'

*

'I want to hear it from you.'

Ellie stared with unwavering grit. She knew where this was going. After twenty years of lying, she had convinced herself it was all just in Tommy's mind but looking at Drew now, knowing that someone else had been allowed into the circle, it became real all over again.

'I want to hear it from the horse's fucking mouth,' he continued, his voice raspy and fraught with menace.

Secrets and lies had woven their way through this place for all these years. It had all begun that one fateful night where she lost her best friend, a night she would forever regret.

'Ellie, I already know. I'm giving you a chance to unburden yourself here. To tell me your version of what happened to Lara.'

'Don't do this, Drew. It won't help you and it won't bring Lara back.'

'But it may bring peace to my family and exonerate a man whose life you destroyed.'

'Chris?'

He looked at her ruefully. 'Exactly.'

'I wouldn't waste my sympathy on him,' she finally said, crossing her legs. 'He might not have done that to Lara but who do you think did everything else round here this past few days.' She paused and then moved forward, almost as if she felt she needed to cover the words from the ears of the world. 'Max,

Darren, your stables.'

He groaned. 'Isn't it enough that you ruined his life once, now you want to blame him for the things that are going on now. I don't think Chris Burns would even know his way back into this village, let alone come here to cause that kind of trouble.'

'He's here,' she said, softly, a smugness passing over her face that negated the seriousness of the current accusations.

Drew wasn't playing though. His expression flattened. 'Oh well, I guess we all have to do things we have to do to claim back our lives. What will you do, Ellie? What will you do to give my mum and dad some closure?'

'Why do we have to, Drew? Nothing has changed. You have a call from Tommy when he was clearly drunk. What exactly does he say I did? You know how I feel about your family and about Lara. None of that has changed.'

He stood, angrily leaning over her, his face now contorted between disbelief and the urge to grab her and squeeze her until the last breath left her body.

'You don't understand. I can't unknow this. You pushed my sister over the side of that boat and left her to drown. You knew he had put something in her drink. Lara didn't do drugs. She didn't need them.'

Panicking, Ellie rose. 'No, I didn't, and I didn't know how much Tommy had laced her drink with. We got into an argument. It was silly, not even worth repeating. I didn't mean to push her, and she was always such a strong swimmer, so I didn't realise she was in trouble until it was too late.'

He was clearly smarting, his face reddening as he pulled away from her, his hands now fashioned into a fist that he looked reluctant to use. 'My mother treated you like one of the family. She's never gotten over Lara, but she still made room for you. You lied to the police. You lied to Max and everyone. You said that you saw Chris push Lara out of the boat after you heard them argue. But you didn't. It was you who pushed her.'

'I didn't give her the drugs. The investigation concluded it was misadventure because of the drugs in her system. That was all on Tommy.'

'Are you fucking listening to yourself?'

He looked like he might lunge forward, and it gave Ellie fear. It was a look she recognised because it was similar to the one that her husband used to wear right before he attacked.

'You killed Tommy,' she finally said.

'Yes,' he whispered. 'And I'd do it again. I came to meet him right after the call, you know. He laughed in my face. It happened right here in this living room. I hadn't intended to kill him, but he laughed in my face. He hated Lara, you know. She broke his heart. Perhaps that's why he took it out on you, Ellie. Maybe because you were the poor sidekick.'

The words stung and she knew that he knew that because Drew wasn't a cruel man. Nor was he vindictive. He'd been driven to murder in the same way she thought she had been, by the act of a man who didn't deserve to live. The expression on his face told her that he regretted being so unkind.

'You need to tell my mum what you did. Everybody will know soon enough anyway. You'd be better to get your side of the story before someone else tells it.'

Ellie had no intention of facing anyone. She was getting out of here tonight, fleeing to her new life with her son and daughter. She'd paid the price over and over again for what happened to Lara. Every slap, every punch, every unyielding verbal assault on her for not being Lara in the first place then, subsequently for not being the one to die in Lara's place. No prison could possibly match the one she'd been living in for two decades. She wasn't going to face Connie, Richie, or anyone else.

'You need to tell them.'

She watched him rise and move to the front door. Then, he stopped.

'If I were you, I'd destroy that knife before the police arrive. I reckon they found the strand of your hair in his blood and that pendant that I stole from your drawer. You know, the one my mother gave you because it belonged to Lara, and you liked it so much.'

Ellie saw him to the door.

He spun round just as he stepped out. 'You were

part of our family. How could you face us all these years?'

'The same way you'll have to face yourself now. Can I ask you one more thing before you go?'

Drew held his hands up, offering her freedom to ask anything she wanted. Against the darkness, his silhouetted was more sinister than she ever remembered it. 'Why seventeen times. The police said Tommy died after the first time. Why was it necessary to do that?'

He let out a sharp sniff. 'One for every year of my sister's life.'

Ellie watched Drew walk away, suspecting she'd never see him again. It was one more figure who she hadn't realised she didn't want in her life until now. Once he was out of sight, she fumbled in her pocket for her mobile handset. She tapped on the screen and then lifted it to her ear.

One deep breath and then she spoke. 'Hi, Maggie. Did you get all of that?'

CHAPTER THIRTY-EIGHT

Connie shrieked as two legs came flying up at her. She suddenly stumbled over the edge of the boat and saw the water reach up to grab her. She was screaming now, a sharp shrill noise that clashed with the explosion of waves as the waters crashed all around her.

The gun was gone. She wasn't sure if it had fallen onto the boat or if it had come into the water with her, but she was now flailing wildly underwater and trying desperately to get to the surface again.

Finally, the dark sky came back into view. She was swimming up, panic subsiding and now glad that she hadn't inebriated herself further. It was hard enough to lose her balance like that. She had to focus because she no longer had the upper hand. As she emerged from the water, she saw he was leaning over, hands free and ready to launch himself at her.

Richie was on the phone though it wasn't clear who he was speaking to.

Simon had kicked the boat away from the edge of

the pier to allow her safe passage back to land. He was leaning over now, arm extended and urging her to rush before Chris finished untying his ankles.

Connie wasn't ready to give up though. If it meant putting her own life in the laps of the Gods, she would at least go to her death knowing it had been on her terms. Besides, she was ready to accept death. because she knew Lara would be there waiting on her. What better reason to be fearless of the one thing everyone feared the most?

She saw Chris stand, his silhouette towering up until it looked like he could touch the clouds. She might not have the gun anymore, but she still had her hands and a little of her fight left in her. So, she grabbed the boat and began to shake it violently.

Chris roared. 'What are you doing, you mad old bitch. Are you trying to kill us both? '

She wouldn't waste her breath arguing. She simply shook it some more until Chris rolled over the edge and deep down into the murky waters. She waited and waited.

Silence enveloped them and she turned to see

that Richie was rushing towards her, arms stretched outwards, and his mobile phone tightly gripped in his hand.

'Connie, come on, give me your hand. Leave him be,' said Richie.

She couldn't though because Connie was a woman of determination. She would finish this. Even if it meant that his body floated up onto the embankment tomorrow. She would take whatever punishment awaited her.

Still, she waited, her hope that he would float to the surface, and she'd know for sure he was dead.

Still, he remained underwater.

A minute had passed. The longest minute she had endured for a long time. Then, she spun round in the water, kicking her legs and feeling the cold.

The rain began, adding just one more unwanted element to the chaos. The surrounding cliffs and hills loomed in the distance, dark and sprawling and a reflection of the valley of torture she continued to endure.

Richie was begging now. 'Come on, Connie. It's

over. He didn't do what you think he did.'

Connie might have been intrigued enough to ask Richie what he meant but, in that moment, she heard and felt movement.

The water shifted slightly, forming a tiny whirlwind until the waves parted.

Out of the centre of it arrived the nemesis of her life. Chris was upon her now, pushing her on her shoulders and pulling her away from the safety of land and that old barely used boat.

Connie didn't know it because she was caught up in the moment, but she was injured. Her blood was leaking but she didn't know where. Had she caught her skin on the boat when she went over. All she knew was that Chris was now in her eyeline and had placed his grubby hands on her.

She looked up again and saw Richie dive in. She hadn't wanted him to help, she had wanted him to get Simon out of there before the police arrived and got involved.

'Stay there,' he was shouting.

She turned back to Chris who was staring her

dead in the face, his eyes ablaze with the same hatred that she herself had known. It was like the two faces of evil staring into each other's void black soul. She grabbed for the side of the boat, hellbent she would finish him. She was relieved to see that the gun was inside. It must have fallen when he'd taken the wind out of her.

Connie reached in and grabbed for the weapon but she felt someone pull her hand away. She lashed out, raining her fist down on Chris's already battered face. She could feel him try to turn her.

'Listen to me. Listen to me,' her husband called.

At that moment, Richie was pulling her away. She had the gun in her hand and was trying to hold tight to it. She couldn't mull over it anymore. She had to do this and finally send him to hell where he belonged.

'He didn't do anything. He's been telling the truth.' Richie, always the voice of reason, was holding her now.

Connie turned to look at Chris and in that moment saw whatever was behind those eyes simply dissipate. It was as if he just needed to hear someone have faith in him. She didn't understand what Richie was saying.

'Oh, Richie, don't be so naive. I know he didn't kill her but he fed her the drugs and then he left her to die. We've always known it wasn't intentional, but does it make any difference?' She could hear herself and she knew that even as she spoke the words, they sounded less and less compelling with each passing syllable.

'No, he actually didn't do any of that. His version of events was the truth. Ellie and Tommy lied.'

Chris's eyes widened. 'Ellie?' He spat out another mouthful of blood, a fresh injury from her lashing out at him.

'What are you talking about? Lied about what.'

Richie shook his head and she saw that grit in his eyes. 'Everything, Con. They lied about everything. They didn't see Chris give our Lara drugs, because it was Tommy who spiked her drink. They also didn't see Chris push her over the edge of the boat because she didn't come to the lake with him. She came with them and got into a fight with Ellie. Ellie pushed her and when they couldn't revive her, they ran.'

'I don't know what you're telling me,' she said, her mind exploding as the last twenty years unraveled. She looked at Chris and shivered. She didn't know how to unhate him.

A moment later her son was helping her out of the water. As she climbed onto the pier, Connie felt herself wane. The air had been knocked out of her and all she wanted to do was lay down and sob. All these years, she'd been staring her daughter's killers in the face, hating the wrong person. Connie had been instrumental in the hate pushed onto Cathy Burns. Now she knew that the woman had died of loneliness and the sudden urge to vomit fell upon her. She retched, words failing her as she watched her two men help Chris back onto the pier. It had been all it took to finally crush Connie into a state of real hysterical madness.

CHAPTER THIRTY-NINE

'Come on lazy girl. Get up.'

Lara felt the duvet being slid off her quickly as the cold settled on her skin. Why was her mother always such a bitch.

'Come on, the brain doesn't educate itself.'

She sighed. 'I can learn just as much not going to school as I can going.'

Connie laughed. 'I know you know everything already; you're only going so I don't get arrested and so I can get into this pigsty of a room.'

'I can clean my own room,' she moaned.

'And yet, here we are. Up!'

Lara finally arrived downstairs forty minutes later, hair in a wild funk, make-up troweled on and denim shorts that barely covered the line of her buttocks. Anything to annoy the woman who had already ruined her day.

'You look pretty,' said Connie, masterful in the art of teenage manipulation.

'This old thing,' said Lara, pulling at the loose t-

shirt that barely covered the naval. 'It won't be on for long.'

Richie choked as he took another bite of his cornflakes. 'No, it won't,' he finally said. 'Go upstairs and put on some clothes that are appropriate for school.'

Connie stepped in. 'Not appropriate for school,' she mocked. 'Richie, you are so old fashioned. Don't you know she's a fashionista.'

He looked at both of them and appeared to opt out. After all, he wouldn't win if they were both pretending to be on the same side. The warfare between mother and teenage daughter was as old as time and was only matched by the utter mutual protectiveness that would kick in later.

Lara eyed them both, neither one taking her on now and decided she might give them a break today. She was going out with Tommy and Ellie tonight and then meeting up with Chris later. Also, she hadn't yet revealed her plans not to do the final year in school and go travelling. That would be another battle that might lead to World War three.

'Dad, could I borrow twenty pounds?'

Richie looked at her in mild irritation. 'Lara, you've got a bank balance that could choke a horse. I know this because it was working with the horses that earned you that money. You said you were saving for something. It can't be that important.'

'A boob job,' she said, enjoying the look on his face.

He quickly dipped into his wallet, his face reddening and handed her a note.

'Okay, I'm away to put my school clothes on,' she finally said, giving Connie a cheeky wink.

Connie laughed, clearly reminded of herself two decades before. The battles lines had been drawn, but the cease fire had been temporarily put in place. The ever-changing hormones of a teenage girl.

She stopped outside and heard the gentle sway of her parents bickering. She'd caused that but she knew their marriage was made of re-enforced steel. It could withstand anything.

'You give into her too easily.'

Richie's voice hardened. 'You were about to let

her go to school looking like a pop star. And not a very classy one. And by the way, get her to stop practicing her make-up techniques on Simon. I don't think he's very comfortable with it.'

CHAPTER FORTY

The gun was gone, and so was Connie.

Richie and Simon were both standing with Chris, cleaning him up despite his insistence that he didn't need their help.

No apology could ever make up for what had happened between them, and Richie suspected forgiveness was now entering its second phase of reluctance. At least this time they were armed with the truth.

'I wasn't planning on anyone dying,' said Chris. 'The gun was for my own protection. I wanted to hold you all captive so that I could make you see what you've done. I'll never get the time back with my mum. You lost Lara just as I did but nobody took your life away from you.'

Richie, still not noticing that his wife was not standing behind him, tried to offer a hand of support to Chris but the man declined.

'Chris. If it's any consolation, your mum tried to reason with us all. I had a great deal of respect for her. She didn't get a fair time, but I hope you know me and the boys tried to help her best we could.'

'It should have been me. You all took that away from me,' said Chris, wearily. Then, he looked past them. 'Where's Connie?'

Simon turned and walked the pier. 'Mum?'

The other men followed but she was nowhere to be seen. She had simply vanished, stealth-like and hadn't said a word to them.

Simon turned back to look at them both, worry contorting his face. 'Her car's gone.'

*

Drew was in handcuffs and in the back seat of the squad car.

Ryan stood by his own vehicle and watched as Maggie comforted Ellie. Ellie also had questions to face. She wasn't leaving here tonight. After all, they had her on record admitting to pushing a girl to her death, however accidental it may have been.

'What you did was the stupid actions of a young jealous woman. I wish you had told someone all those years ago. You might have had a different life and so might he. I doubt he'll get off with a slap on the wrist.'

'I'm not sure I want him to get a slap on the wrist. He was about to let me take the blame for killing Tommy.'

Maggie blew into the air. 'Then, maybe you'll have some idea of how Chris has felt all these years. I doubt it though.' She walked away, barely able to contain her contempt. She had fought that girl's corner. She could never really look at Ellie the same again.

Ryan watched with interest. Someone had finally broken Maggie's temper and it turned out to be the one person who he wouldn't have suspected. 'That was harsh.'

'Not as harsh as she deserves. She'll go on with her life probably. A slap on the wrist because, despite my anger at her, I believe she was still a victim.'

Ryan ran his finger along the metal of his car. 'You almost sound like you grudge her it.'

'I don't know if I do. She's a nice girl but she's weak and she's allowed all this to play out around her without ever telling the truth. So many people have lost so much and all because she couldn't stand up for herself or her friend. I get it but I don't like it. I think leaving here will be the best thing for her and all concerned.'

'Like I said, harsh. And that's coming from me.'

She laughed then, a little break in the somber mood. 'I'll get over it and so will you. I don't know about him though.'

Just as Maggie looked up at the squad car to look at Drew, she found herself looking at Connie pushing the glass window. There was no mistaking the devastation on her face and Maggie found herself wondering just how much Connie knew.

Then, she saw the exchange of looks between Connie and Ellie and she knew there was no more hiding for Ellie.

CHAPTER FORTY-ONE

The gunshot fired through the air. There was an inordinate amount of silence surrounding them all. Nobody screamed, nor darted dramatically. They all just stood perfectly still and watched as Ellie Hunter went down.

She was dead before her body crashed to the ground and Connie was already throwing the weapon to the ground. The sirens flared as a uniformed officer ran to her side. Someone else moved towards Ellie, trying to catch her ahead of her fall but it was too late.

Maggie watched as if she were watching a movie, disbelief that her little village had escalated to this level of violence. She looked outwards. The cliffs, the lakes, the rising spires of houses all looked the same. The landscape had changed though.

She heard Connie scream, the scream of a woman who had been forced over the edge. All those years of erroneously directed hatred had to go somewhere. In the end, it had gone in the form of a little steel bullet straight into the body of a girl

Connie had treated as her own.

Maggie's heart ached. Despite her harsh words, she would never have wished this for Ellie, nor her beautiful children. She turned away to cry then. She couldn't look anymore because it had just become too gut wrenching to witness.

Did any of these people know what they'd done to each other? How could love be so destructive?

She refused the comforting hand of Detective Starling because she knew it made him awkward and she didn't want this moment to get any more difficult. So, she walked away, biting each tear as it landed on her lips. She just wanted to run and get away from here. The truth was out but it hadn't released anyone, and it hadn't made a damn bit of difference to all the lives that it had destroyed.

*

Connie closed her eyes and heard the soft whisper of her daughter's voice. It was over now, she wanted to say but she knew that wasn't true. This was only the start of a new whole other heartbreak. She feared that Chris would tell the police what Simon did. Right now, though, her terror lay in wait for what would happen to Drew.

She opened her eyes. From across the street, with sheets of glass between them, Connie could see his frightened tearstained face. She held up her cuffed hands and pressed the tip of her thumb and index finger together and ran it across the front of her lips. She shook her head. A warning to him to say nothing. She might be going to jail but she was not taking her family with her.

EPILOGUE I

The escalator rumbled beneath his feet as he left behind the craziest days of his life. Was it possible he had finally found closure? He no longer felt the weight of anger that had crushed down on him for so long. There was a lightness to his thoughts as he realised that there had been a reason beyond the realms of his understanding that he had to go back home and do what he had done. Perhaps just the right amount of justice had been served. After all, he believed now that the Gibbs family had been as much a victim of lies as he had. They had perpetrated hatred upon him all those years ago because they believed he had committed the most heinous act against their beloved daughter. In turn, he believed they had perpetrated an act upon him that had led to his mother's suicide.

Chris no longer knew where his sorrow lay. Lara had been taken far too soon but her absence had permitted other gifts. He longed, achingly, for a second chance with his mother but he knew it would never be and all he could do was forgive her and himself. Mostly though, he suspected the sorrow he truly felt might relate to the loss of twenty years of his life. Not because of what Max McDermott had done, though it certainly had an impact. Not even in relation to how the Gibbs had treated him and his mother. The sorrow he felt lay within himself for all those wasted years.

He saw someone familiar up ahead and he smiled. He instantly felt a momentary regret because he had never allowed anyone to get too close. Yet, the woman standing at the arrivals gate wore a gleaming smile in preparation for his arrival. Another apology owed because Julia had been the one solid in his life over these past years and he had never appreciated it until now. She had supported his quest for closure, even when she didn't agree with it. She had even east by his side as he stalked cyber space in search of the data he needed to exorcise those past demons. She had never faltered, never judged. Any words that passed her lips were always of concern and kindness.

He moved a little quicker, backpack carrying all

the little trinkets of his childhood. There were a few photos, one of Cathy that he liked and that would now adorn the fireplace. No finer person would be immortalised there.

Chris returned the smile. He whispered a hello, felt himself get teary and then put his one good arm round her back. He pulled her in and kissed her on the lips and for the first time there was no guilt that he had moved on. Lara would approve of Julia. So would his mother, he was sure. 'When is this coming off?' She pulled at the beard just enough that it tugged but didn't hurt.

'Today. Now that I got what I went for, I don't have to hide behind masks.'

Chris looked down just int one to feel a gentle pull on his leg. 'Daddy, did you bring me a holiday toy?' The youngest of his three kids waited to be swept up in his arms.

'No toys form holiday, baby girl. But let's get out of here and maybe we can get something on the way home.'

The little girl beamed, locking onto his hand.

Meanwhile his two boys made their mark at his side, each one a miniature replica of the person he used to be. Chris had everything and he had almost lost it to an unnecessary quest. The briefest flashback of Ellie came to mind, but he bushed it away. Then, Connie's voice echoed in his mind. Not words of bitterness though. Instead, she was wishing him well just as she had from the jail cell that morning when he'd begged to be allowed to see her. It was humbling to think that he wanted to kill her with his own hands and now, knowing she was locked away for years, he felt quite sorry for her.

The thoughts didn't linger.

Chris led his beautiful family, finally free of his past, out into the concourse and waited to be cabbed home. There, he could finally leave Lara and the curse of Crianlarich behind and finally focus on his own life.

EPILOGUE II

The moment had finally arrived. As Connie walked through the prison gates, her heart thudded with a mixture of fear and excitement. She had been waiting long enough for this moment, wading through a bright ugly clarity for it all to be over. Everything seemed just a little duller out here. That was okay because she had lived her life under a bright spotlight for five years. Now, dread filled, she wondered what lay ahead.

The ride to her new place was quiet, and Connie couldn't help but think of how much her life had changed since that night. She wasn't who she used to be. She had learned to meditate her anger away. Where she used to think of her daughter, Lara, in fits and bursts, she could now reduce the impact on her consciousness. She was free, but the thought of starting this new chapter in her life was overwhelming.

Finally, Connie arrived at the address she had been given. A train trundled over the bridge above her as she stood at the foot of the four tall block sandstone and smiled. She had never been a city girl, but she had also never been a convicted killer of two people before. At least here she would be anonymous. She climbed the stairs, an overpowering whiff of bleach reaching her nostrils as she unlocked the storm door on the first floor.

Outside, Partick Cross was heaving with people hustling between work, shopping, and idle socialising. Once, Connie might have suspected they all had the perfect untouched lives. Such was the freedom of their movement. She knew better now because she, herself, had lived a life that was mostly a lie. No person knew the art of deceit better than she.

She rested on a bed that was more comfortable than anything she'd slept on for years. She sniffed at the scent drifting through the coffee machine. She touched a mobile phone that would allow her free access to the world, a freedom she could never take for granted again. She looked at the screen wistfully. How easy it would be to go back to her old life and nest in Richie's arms. She could live that life; she just couldn't live with herself.

Connie must have drifted. She was just settling into a daydream when she was startled by a knock at the door. Surely it wasn't time for her parole visit already, she thought, rising from the bed in a nark.

She opened the door with a heavy sigh and found Richie standing there on the doorstep. That old familiar smile, handsome and commanding, she used to be mesmerised by it. That was old Connie. This Connie was hardened to the charms of a man. Even Richie.

'Aren't you going to invite me in?'

'Sure,' she replied, burying any enthusiasm that might threaten to surface.

He sauntered in, nodding his head. 'I spoke to your parole officer. She said you have to check in with her at least once a week.'

Connie nodded back. She wasn't really in the mood for small talk. Nor did she want to have any meaningful conversation with Richie. She had made her decision when in prison. Back then, she thought she had another eight years to serve. She didn't want him waiting. She didn't want her boys waiting. She wanted them to go on with their lives. Now, she didn't dare to ask about them because she wanted them to get on with life without her, she just didn't want to know that they had. 'What are you doing here, Richie?'

'Is that anyway of greeting your husband?'

She sniffed. 'Ex-husband.'

'Not yet,' he declared. 'Not until I agree, and I don't agree. I've waited for you to come out for five years. Can't you give me something to work with?'

'I can't go back to that village,' she snapped.

Richie retreated, walked towards the warm coffee pot, and poured himself a mug. 'Want some?'

She shook her head. She didn't want coffee, nor did she want him to have coffee. That would suggest he could stay a while and that would only make her decision harder to enforce.

'You know, I've wanted to make some changes to my life for a long time. The thing that happened with Lara, then all that revenge stuff, it left a nasty taste.'

Connie drew her eyes up. So, this is where this visit was heading.

'Not that I'm saying any of it was your fault. You did what you did out of love for our daughter. Truth is, Con. I'm only half alive without you. I need you.'

'I can't come back,' she repeated, less convincingly.

'Good, because I don't want to go back either. I've put the house on the market. The estate agent thinks it will sell quickly and then we can buy a place down here. Nobody will know us. We can start again.'

She wondered if he had been knocked on the head. Her story had been all over the media. Even if she wasn't recognised by many, she suspected someone would know who she was. 'It won't work. Too much water under the bridge.'

'It's already done. I've spoken to your parole officer, and we can move you as soon as we have a place that is suitable for both of us.'

Connie wondered if she closed her eyes, would he be gone in a puff of smoke? It was likely she was dreaming this fantasy up for herself because deep down, it sounded perfect. It also sounded insane to her right now.

He reached for her, pulled her into his strong arms and rocked her gently. 'The last twenty odd years have been a limbo. First, the grief. Then, the wait to get to the truth. And the last five years have been hell without you. Now, we have a chance to finally make a clean break of it. Say you will give it a chance.'

'What about the boys? What will they say if you up sticks and run away with me.'

He laughed gently. 'Who's running? For the first time in years, neither of us are running from anything. The boys have their own thoughts. I'll let them tell you those, though.'

Narrowing her eyes, she moved backwards. 'What?'

'They're outside waiting on the word. You didn't think I was coming here alone when I could come armed with them. Go, look for yourself.'

Connie rushed to the window, pulled back the net

curtain and looked across the street. She saw Simon and Drew instantly. Then, she saw her seven-year-old grandson walk between them. Connie had opted for a life where her heart would be an empty contraption, serving only as a vehicle to pump blood. She thought she would never feel full again. For the first time in years, her heart bettered her mind and she found herself weeping. Just seeing them all again, maybe there was a chance of her being happy again. She turned back to Richie. 'I'm frightened.'

He reached for her again, this time holding her tightly. 'Me too, sweetheart. It's less scary if we're together, though.'

She looked at him and recognised that her absence had allowed him to grow. He looked genuinely content, and he was standing up to her. It was refreshing.

The decision was made. She couldn't fight it. It was all she had wanted for long enough. The only thing standing in her way was herself. So, she pressed her nose against his chest and finally accepted what would be. In her mind, she stepped out of her own way and wasted not another minute questioning her right to happiness.

THE END

Printed in Great Britain
by Amazon

26350861R00188